Tremble

SIGNIFICANT BROTHERS #6

E. DAVIES

Publisher's Note: This is a work of fiction. Names, characters, places, and incidents are a product of the author's imagination. Locales and public names are sometimes used for atmospheric purposes. Any resemblance to actual people, living or dead, or to businesses, companies, events, institutions, or locales is completely coincidental.

Tremble / E. Davies. – 1st ed.
ISBN: 978-1-912245-17-8

Tremble

Prologue

EVAN

"WE'VE GOT TIME BEFORE THAT LEO GUY ARRIVES."

Although Evan said it in his most suggestive tone, it seemed to take Monty a few moments to realize what he meant.

"Oh. Yeah, we have time." Monty sounded tired. After the drive from New York, no wonder. They'd done it in two six-hour days, but Monty wouldn't let Evan switch off with him and drive.

He couldn't have Monty all tired out before their week of dude ranch fun even began. Evan grinned and leaned in closer. "And there aren't many people around right now. They must be all out on trail rides and stuff."

"No," Monty agreed, raising a brow. He sounded half-interested now, at least. "What did you have in mind?"

"Why don't we take a wander around the place? I bet I can find a ride of my own." Evan squeezed Monty's ass, then flicked off the light in their cabin. "Out we go."

"Cool," Monty grinned. If Evan didn't know him, he would have found it weird that the smile never seemed to go to his eyes. But he did, so he didn't take it personally. Monty had a stressful job, after all, and a lot on his mind. Hence the romantic getaway to a dude ranch near Knoxville.

Finally, a week with just the two of them. No family, no job, no distractions or excuses. And Evan planned to make the most of it before they had to return to reality.

"You think they'll be fine with… you know… us?"

"I'm not gonna bend over in the stocks in front of everyone," Evan laughed. "Some gay guy owns the place anyway. Come on. Where's your spirit of adventure?"

Teasing Monty was risky. Sometimes it worked, and sometimes it just pissed him off. Luckily, today, it worked.

"Fine," Monty hummed and strode for the cabin door. "Let's go, before we run out of time."

Evan followed in his wake, much like always. Tailing after him seemed to be his lot in life, but it wasn't bad as far as life paths went.

"There's a barn."

Evan smirked. "Hay loft?"

"That sounds high up," Monty said, narrowing his eyes. "We're not gonna fall, are we?"

"I won't let you fall," Evan promised, grinning. "Except into bliss."

"Bliss beats broken arms." Monty wandered alongside Evan until they reached the barn, which was well downwind of the cabins. They both glanced around and listened, and after catching no glimpse or sound of anyone nearby, they slipped in.

It was easy for Evan to find a way up. Monty, in his fancy city boy trousers and shirt, needed a bit more persuasion, but when they finally tumbled onto the floor together, it was worth it.

Evan hadn't had this much fun in bed with Monty... well... ever.

He tried to push the thought aside. They had years of their lives together to experiment and explore and keep things fresh.

"Come on," he whispered, crawling away from the ladder. They could still clearly hear if anyone walked down the wooden boards along the aisles of the barn, but they would be just out of eyeshot. All he needed was fifteen minutes.

Monty wrinkled his nose as he shuffled along the boards, through the perfectly clean hay. "They're gonna know we were sneaking around," he whispered back.

"I'll dust you off." Evan grabbed him by the shirt front and hauled him in for a kiss to distract him from all the reasons he was coming up with why this was a bad idea. Replacing them with some reasons it was a good idea was a way more efficient use of their time.

Monty moaned softly. He suddenly seemed more amenable to the idea. He grabbed Evan's shoulder and manhandled him onto his back, then straddled him.

Evan's heart raced as he worked Monty's zipper down and unbuttoned his trousers. No way would Monty fuck him here—he'd barely agreed to get up here—but blowjobs weren't out of the question.

He giggled as Monty shuffled awkwardly up his body, but his mouth was soon too full to make any comments. Monty wasted no time pushing his half-hard cock into Evan's mouth. Evan let his warm tongue lap around and under the shaft, bobbing his head as best he could at this angle.

Monty took over before long, thrusting into his mouth hard and fast. He stifled his gasps of pleasure when Evan swallowed around the head of his cock, but Evan could still clearly hear them.

"I'm gonna come in your mouth, baby," Monty told him.

Just then, they both froze. There were voices nearby the barn, and they were getting closer.

"—the ride tomorrow?"

"No, I'll handle it. I think there's just six guests," another man answered the question.

Heavy footsteps trod the boards beneath them, and they both caught their breath. Monty was frozen in place, his throbbing shaft deep in Evan's mouth. With Monty straddling his chest, Evan couldn't see anything, but his ears were keenly tuned for signs of the men coming up the ladder.

They didn't.

"We'll make sure Mary gets the day off, then. None of them reported prior experience. I don't know about the couple who just came down from New York."

Their conversation continued as they walked through the barn until their voices faded.

Evan tried not to giggle around Monty's cock, and he squeezed his ass lightly to encourage him.

Monty fucked his mouth fast and hard now, his grip tight in Evan's hair. He was silent, except for his heavy breathing. Even his weight was carefully distributed so he didn't shift and make the boards creak.

They could still make out the other men's voices, if not what they were saying, and it was all Evan could do not to laugh.

Hiding in the hay loft until they left wasn't going to be very dignified, but at least they were passing the time in pleasure.

Monty came, thick and hot on Evan's tongue and

straight down his throat. Luckily, Evan knew how to swallow without choking or coughing, and he sucked Monty dry.

Monty breathed in and out, as if calming himself down, and pulled back. He shifted slowly to keep the creak quiet, then zipped his cock back into his trousers.

Evan grinned and squeezed himself pointedly, but Monty scowled. "Really?" Monty whispered.

"What?" They hadn't been caught yet. May as well make the most of it.

Monty jerked his chin toward the ladder. "They're far enough away now. We can get out."

"Gonna leave me hanging?"

"You bet I fucking will." Monty hissed. "I'm not getting my ass arrested for... indecency, or whatever. In Tennessee!" He scooted over to the ladder and slithered to the ground, then slipped out the barn door as Evan craned his neck to watch.

Evan rolled his eyes. Even getting a great blowjob hadn't fixed Monty's attitude. Was he really that tired from the drive?

He made his own move and got out undetected, though his heart raced anyway. This was probably the most daring thing he'd done in his life. By the time he was clear of the barn, he spotted Monty waiting for him, arms folded, by the end of the nearest row of cabins.

"Hey," Evan greeted with a grin as if it had been hours.

Monty just eyed him with displeasure, which wasn't fun to try to ignore. This was his new normal, though. Evan couldn't do much right these days. When Monty got home from work, even when Evan had a nice meal ready, he found something to complain about.

Apparently, the honeymoon period was a lie. They'd only just gotten engaged, and already, the glow had worn off.

That was the other reason they were here: their engagement photo shoot.

Evan picked a few bits of hay off Monty's trousers and shirt, then grinned. "Safe and sound," he told him. "As promised." He leaned in to try for a kiss.

Monty turned his face away and strode for the cabin.

Evan reeled, his feet rooted in place as he watched his fiancé's retreating back.

Hopefully, this Leo guy could work a miracle. Monty had always been good at playing happy for the camera, but Evan was starting to wonder whether that would hold.

God, his blue balls were killing him.

It's gonna be a long afternoon.

CHAPTER
One

JOSH

It was impossible not to notice the happy couple.

Josh wasn't even pretending he wasn't jealous. He would never in his life admit it to his best friends, but in the privacy of his own head? Yeah, his eyes were a little too green.

One of the guys from New York looked elegant but cold, in a ruthless businessman way. The other was… well, he was downright gorgeous. He had an eager, quick smile. Though he trailed after his fiancé like he was used to being in his shadow, he could have held Josh's attention… if only they weren't here for an engagement photo shoot.

Good for them. And Josh didn't need to be jealous. It wasn't like he had the time for a fiancé anyway.

Josh flipped shut the schedule book now that he was confident all the activities were covered tomorrow. All he had to worry about was Adam, the kid who was supposed to be running the ranch shop. He'd been mysteriously absent on the last few sunny days, and tomorrow had a great forecast.

So did today—good for the engagement shoot. Honeymooning couples, and those newly engaged, often stayed here.

One of Josh's friends, Leo, ran a photography business. He specialized in wedding photography for same-sex couples, portraits of trans people, and that kind of stuff. His big thing was making photography accessible to people who weren't often seen by society as beautiful, pure, sweet, or even real.

It was only natural to work with Leo, offering the space on his farm as a backdrop. In the Smoky Mountains nearby, rhododendrons rewarded the photographer and client who were willing to hike. Lower down, right here, fields of black-eyed Susans, sourwood trees, and witchhazel bloomed as the seasons marched on. There was always a pretty backdrop.

The deliberately cultivated rustic charm of the farm buildings offered plenty of backdrop options for those looking for a Wild West feeling.

They had a mutually beneficial agreement where Leo referred guests to stay on Josh's farm, and Josh offered photo shoots by Leo to his customers. A lot of people got great pictures of happy family memories and a memorable vacation, and everyone won.

The constant coming and going of guests kept Josh busy year-round. The late August rush of people hurrying to get vacations in before school started was finally slowing down. It was back to fewer families and more newlyweds. Josh wrinkled his nose.

On the other hand, it was gratifying to host people who often felt uncertain or wary about public displays of affection. It was an incredible opportunity to get to give them a safe place to enjoy a vacation together without having to pretend not to be together. Josh had carefully made this ranch somewhere they could hold hands or lean on each other or even touch without glares or worse.

"Hey, bud," Leo greeted as he swung into Josh's office from the doorframe. His camera bag over his shoulder, a bucket hat firmly jammed on, he looked like he was ready for a safari. "Have you seen my clients?"

"The hot ones?" Josh grinned. "Yeah, they were wandering around the farm earlier, probably looking at spots."

"I said to meet me in the main building." Leo glanced out to the desk. "Actually, I think I see one of them now."

"Good luck!" Josh called after Leo as he barreled out. He grinned. It was kind of funny watching him at work. He was so clearly passionate about what he did.

That passion was hard for Josh to keep up sometimes. It so often felt like the same shit on different days. Did all hotel owners get so jaded? Maybe he just needed to get laid… or date.

Hah. Like he'd be able to trust some random guy he'd just met enough to date him. Grindr was fine, but more? Dating just wasted his time when he tried it.

Speaking of time, he didn't have much to spare today. They didn't harvest a lot—it was less of a working farm than a small-scale operation tailored to impress tourists. Still, he couldn't let the farm hands spend *all* day flirting with the guests.

"Josh?" That was Ryanna, his front desk guru. "Got a minute?" That was their code phrase for *help me out, this customer's an asshole.*

"Of course." Josh followed her out to the reception desk. "I'm Josh. Pleasure to meet you," he introduced himself.

"Montgomery Ray Charles."

Oh, God. Anyone who introduced himself with his middle name was a guaranteed dick. Josh suddenly felt bad for the brand-new fiancé who was waiting outside with Leo, their voices faintly audible.

Josh kept the smile on his face and nodded. "What can I do for you, Montgomery?"

"Oh, please. Monty."

Josh already kind of wanted to throttle him. "Monty, my apologies."

"I'd like to check out early."

And, let me guess. He's prepaid. He threw Ryanna a look, and she nodded. "That won't be a problem, sir."

"And I'd like a refund for the other six nights."

"Ah. Well, have you prepaid, or was this a walk-up booking?"

Monty waved a hand imperiously. "Oh, I don't know. My people took care of it. But I have to leave early for business. I'm sure you'll have *no* trouble renting out a..." he paused before continuing, "lovely little place like this."

Ooh, he was trying to bait Josh. But he wasn't going to rise to it. "Well, our payment terms say any money paid is nonrefundable." On the other hand, this guy looked like he was dripping with money. That meant lawyers and banks getting involved, and he didn't have time for that crap. "We wouldn't want to ruin your engagement celebrations, though. Let me see what we can do."

"Thank you," Monty said, but in a tone that made it clear he'd expected that answer. He turned on his heel.

"Checkout's at noon tomorrow," Josh said to his back, rolling his eyes at Ryanna. Once the guy was gone, he clapped her shoulder. "Let me guess. He went all *I want to speak to the manager* on you."

"Yeah. He turned a lot nicer when you walked in," she said, gritting her jaw for a moment before she took a deep breath. "Hopefully the trail ride later goes well, and he doesn't get saddle sores."

Josh grinned. "Those *were* prepaid separately, though. Part of the package. It would be a shame if he didn't get that back."

"Wouldn't it?" Ryanna tapped on the keyboard and settled into her chair again. "Want me to refund the rest of the stay?"

"Go for it. I'd rather have him the hell elsewhere than being an ass to you," Josh said, shaking his head. It just went to show that they were no different from straight folks. Dicks were dicks inside and out.

Josh watched as Monty swept Leo up in his presence and marched him along, a hand on his shoulder.

Monty's fiancé trailed after them, his posture subdued, even though he'd been actively chatting with Leo a few moments ago. Josh tightened his jaw as he watched.

Dicks sure were dicks, and if there was one thing he'd learned in life, it was this: there was nothing he could do about it.

CHAPTER

Two

EVAN

Evan had a lot of practice smiling for the camera, even when he wanted to curl up in a corner and forget the world.

But despite Leo's guidance and Evan's coaxing, Monty was still being weirdly distant. Once again, nothing Evan did seemed to be good enough.

And this was the damn engagement shoot, which Monty had wanted more than Evan did, for his company and family and all that crap. It looked good for his business to be in a stable, Instagram-worthy relationship. He had a family who sent out email newsletters on their spoiled little kids' private school progress. Engagement photos were a must for Monty.

"Hey, babe," Evan teased, tickling Monty's side. He usually gave in and smiled at Evan when he did that, but instead, Monty glared and stepped back.

Even Leo paused, lowering his camera slightly.

Embarrassment curled Evan's stomach into knots, and he felt himself tense up. "What's wrong? Feeling okay?"

"Just work on the brain," Monty mumbled, not making eye contact.

The guy Evan had seen him talking to earlier in the office walked past, offering the three of them a friendly nod. "How's it going?" He clapped Leo's shoulder like he knew him.

He was cute as hell, in the country boy kind of way that meant he didn't even know it. And he actually remembered how to smile in a way that looked like he meant it.

Was he with Leo? Evan was instantly a tiny bit jealous.

"Fine, thanks." Monty's tone was cool.

"Everything's taken care of, as we discussed," the other guy—an employee here, then?—said. He glanced at Evan and smiled, flashing wonderful white teeth. "Sorry you couldn't make it for the week, but I hope you guys enjoy your night. Let me know if I can do anything."

Evan blinked a few times. Couldn't make it for the week? "Thanks," he answered after a moment to hide his confusion. He was used to not knowing what was going on anyway.

Monty stepped away from him even further and nodded jerkily as the other guy strode past them.

Leo stepped away, scrolling through his photos and looking around, shading his eyes as he looked over the fields. It was as clear a *talk this out* signal as Evan could imagine.

"Can't make it?" Evan murmured to Monty.

Monty folded his arms. "Work called. Gotta head back tomorrow."

"Oh." Evan was getting pretty damn used to that, but they'd agreed to at least take a week away from that crap… hadn't they? "But… we said this week…" he trailed off.

"Well, that's life." Monty looked at him, his expression strangely aggressive. "You gotta get used to that if you're joining the family."

Evan raised his eyebrows. "Am I?"

"You can't just get an easy ride in life, you know."

Whoa. Where the hell had *that* come from?

Evan no longer worked for the ad agency where he'd met Monty. He'd never been comfortable selling unhealthy lifestyles to people in exchange for his thirty pieces of silver. When Monty had come along and laughed at his salary, it had been an obvious choice to quit the job and live with him, reducing his expenses to… nothing.

He'd spent the last couple years building Monty's image and brand and goddamn business. It wasn't like he was sitting around at home doing nothing all day.

"And you can't treat me like everything I've done is a hobby." Coming up with press kits wasn't Evan's idea of a relaxing night in. It might not have come with the same risk as running the company, but it was a job. An unpaid one, moreover.

"Our bank account sure says it is."

Evan raised his eyebrows. "Are you saying I don't know shit, or I don't do shit?"

He was so angry he wanted to shake Monty by the shirt, but Leo was already valiantly ignoring their argument, wandering off even further toward the fields.

"Either way," Evan continued, not letting Monty answer yet, "you seem to want these photos to look like *fifteen years married and he just farted in the bed*, not engagement photos."

"I don't give a fuck about the photos."

Evan scoffed. Monty had wanted professional photos taken since the proposal—over dinner at a fancy Italian place in Manhattan—two months ago. He'd kept complaining about not having time, and Evan had basically had to drag him out here. "Yeah, you do. You wanted pictures for your goddamn Instagram."

"Someone told me I was supposed to give a shit about that."

"Oh, so now I *am* working for you?" Evan knew it was a jab, but he didn't care. He was getting pissed off that Monty seemed to treat the whole thing like a joke. He'd never been romantic towards Evan, but he'd at least *tried*. Until now.

"You're ruining the mood," Monty said calmly, jabbing his thumb at Leo.

Evan took a deep breath and let it out, then glared. "At least it won't be fake, like the rest of your goddamn life."

He'd never been one for Monty's lifestyle of dinners with famous or rich people, vacations in the Hamptons, whatever. But he'd at least kept his distance and it had worked.

Until now. He was about to marry into it, and he wasn't entirely sure it wasn't the stupidest move he'd ever made.

"You know what? If you're not committed to this, why fucking bother?" Monty folded his arms again.

Evan glared. "I'm starting to feel the same way. Are you committed to *us*?"

"Not if you're gonna screw up the rest of my life."

"By loving you?" Evan exclaimed. "Or at least *trying*? You make it pretty damn hard some days, you know."

Monty snorted. "Sure. Or loving my money."

How fucking dare he?

Evan held his left hand up so Monty looked at it, then yanked the ring off. "You know, I thought you'd changed. When you gave me this, I thought you were realizing what matters in life. But I'm never, ever going to be first in your life, am I?"

Half of him hoped Monty would beg him to put the ring back on. The other half—and he felt horrible for it—hoped he wouldn't.

Monty snatched it out of his hand. "Yeah. Glad you've realized that. Wish you'd done it six months ago and saved me all this hassle. We're going home now, not tomorrow."

The anger burning through Evan's veins made him shake. "Fucking go without me."

"I'll forward your possessions on Monday," Monty said, and just like that, Evan heard his business-deal voice kick in.

Like they hadn't lived together for three years, and dated for even longer. Like he hadn't quit his career to support Monty's. Like he was… nothing.

A business partner he could screw over. Monty didn't talk work much, but Evan had been starting to suspect he wasn't the best guy to deal with.

God, he wished he'd listened to that gut feeling earlier.

Evan started to laugh, and he found he couldn't stop. *Forward my possessions? What possessions? He paid for everything. And to what address?*

"You never stop laughing," Monty fired at him, turning on his heel to stride away the way Evan had seen him walk away from other people before. "God, I hated that."

Haughty, arrogant, petty. Needing to get the last word in. God, why didn't I see it? I thought he was just stressed, that I could help. That something would change.

Evan sank down to sit on the rusty wheel that had clearly been carefully placed here for the aesthetic appeal.

"Are you okay?"

It took Evan a moment to remember that anyone else was there.

Right. Leo.

"Sorry," Evan mumbled. He'd done it for so long that he didn't even realize he was kicking into *damage control for Monty* mode until he was halfway through his sentence. "I assume you were prepaid, and if not..." *He'll get his people to take care of it.*

"It's already settled," Leo told him gently, crouching next to him. "Anything you need?"

Evan laughed again, weakly. *An ex-fiancé who isn't the biggest dick in the country?* "Just the mini-bar. Sorry for wasting your time." He rose to his feet to head for his cabin, trying to keep it together.

The strangest mix of emotions was flooding through him, and he wasn't sure he could handle them all at once.

It wasn't even anger, depression, denial, any of that grief stuff.

Evan was suddenly terrified of a future—alone, with no job lined up and no place to live—and yet, against all the odds, his heart was light.

No more changing Monty moods to manage. No feeling guilty over spending Monty's money, even when Monty's success over the last few years was down to him.

No more business with boyfriends, that was for damn sure.

The ring off his finger was like a yoke off his shoulders. Evan was a free man.

The mini-bar didn't have nearly enough in it to deal with this situation, but it was still too much for Evan, who had barely eaten today and didn't feel much like trying now.

The mix of vodka, whiskey, and gin miniatures he'd just downed, one after another, couldn't be good for his stomach. He lay very still on the bed, but even that was miserable. The room was spinning now. He wasn't sure if it was better to keep moving or to lie still. Lying still only made everything move more.

A knock sounded on the door.

"Fuck off," Evan muttered. Monty *would* be the type to come back and make him beg for forgiveness.

Another knock.

Evan raised his voice and shouted, "If that's you coming to offer me another chance…" He pushed himself off the bed, staggering to the door. "You can take that chance…" He unlocked it and tugged, but the door wouldn't open. "And shove it…" He unlocked it again, this time sliding the lock the right way. "Up your—"

Oh, shit.

The man on Evan's doorstep wasn't Monty at all.

He clung to the frame, barely keeping himself upright as the room spun and his stomach seemed to keep pace with it.

It was the hot guy from earlier, who'd kind of started the whole fight by saying… what? They weren't staying the week?

Shit. Evan had the sinking feeling that Monty had *planned* this.

The guy was holding a bottle of whisky, but he half-hid it behind his back. "You all right?"

"I'm…"

Evan couldn't stop it in time. Bile rose in his throat, and he doubled over, staggering to his knees.

He threw up.

Almost on the guy's shoes, if he hadn't stepped backward so quickly.

Oh. My. God.

Evan coughed, his eyes burning nearly as much as his

throat. He choked and covered his face, trying to pull himself together.

He told himself to pretend that it was one of Monty's parties where he'd been downing champagne all evening and had to meet some bigwig family friend.

It didn't work. He stayed on his knees, pressing his cheek against the door frame.

This was probably the second-worst day of his life—and only *second*-worst because one day, long ago, he'd agreed to date that asshole.

"I'm Josh. Come on, let's get you inside."

Josh wasn't just hot. He was sweet. And he was gentle as he helped Evan stand and shuffle over to sit on the bed. And he didn't act impatient or angry or any of the ways Monty would have acted when he sat next to Evan, and Evan cried on his shoulder.

Okay. This *was* the worst day of his life.

CHAPTER
Three

JOSH

"You got the rest of the week paid for here," Josh lied, hoping Evan didn't spot the guilt on his face. He was a shitty liar, but the lie was for a good cause. Josh could spare one cabin, which would just sit empty anyway.

It was hard not to feel bad for the guy.

Leo had come straight to the office, looking distraught. No wonder, too. A couple breaking up in the middle of his engagement photo shoot? Leo might have been in war zones, but never one like this. It was Josh's damn fault for mentioning they were leaving early.

Meanwhile, Monty had fled. Before Leo even got to the office, Monty had peeled out of there like a bat out of hell.

Josh had told Leo to take off, and promised he'd look in on Evan later. It seemed kindest to give him a couple hours by himself to call friends or family and get through the shock before dropping by with a bottle of whiskey. Just as a neighbor, offering to talk.

"Okay. If you don't kick me out. I didn't mean to puke on your shoes," Evan moaned, covering his face. He was flat on his back on the bed now, looking like he wanted to melt into the floor.

Josh laughed. "It happens, dude. No worse than my brothers have done."

Evan turned his head slightly. "You got brothers?" He seemed desperate for any subject of conversation that wasn't his breakup, and Josh sympathized.

"Well, technically, no. Only child here. But I got a bunch of guys I met in high school. We call each other brothers now. Most of them—well, all of them but me, actually—have boyfriends now."

Evan just about sat up, and then clearly changed his mind on whether that was a good idea before Josh could intervene. "They're all gay?"

"Yeah. I'm bi, in case your bi-dar doesn't function," Josh added, his lips quirking into a smile.

"Oh. You're not the owner, are you?"

Josh nodded, wondering why Evan wanted to know. "I'm the one who thought running a dude ranch was a great idea, yeah."

"Right. There was something online about... a gay owner."

Josh picked a thread out of his jeans, looking up at the moving ceiling fan. "I say gay sometimes, when people ask. It's simple enough for most people to understand. You'd think bi is, too, but..."

Evan laughed abruptly. "Yeah."

"I have enough problems without trying to teach everyone the 101, you know?" Josh shook his head.

He was pretty sure he wasn't supposed to say that. He was supposed to be willing to educate everyone under the sun at a whim, but he'd never been that type. Some of his brothers, maybe. Not him.

"You have enough problems without looking after some drunk asshole," Evan said with a quiet, self-conscious laugh.

God, even when he should have been taking the time to mope, he was too afraid of being a burden. Josh knew the feeling, and it cut to the bone.

"It's my pleasure," Josh said softly, resting a hand on his arm. "I was gonna bitch about your asshole ex with you over whiskey, but..."

"I got to the mini-bar first," Evan finished, laughing. He finally pushed himself upright, and though Josh steadied him with a hand on his arm, he seemed better-off. "Stomach's better now. I'm sobering up."

"Christ, was that all you had?" Josh squinted at the table of empty miniatures. Looked like he'd downed all four, probably one after the other. "Lightweight."

Evan laughed again. The sound was quiet and hoarse, but it was better than seeing him miserable. "On an empty stomach."

"I'll bring you something," Josh said immediately. He could grab something from the store, or from his own place. What did he have in the fridge?

Evan's brows furrowed. "You don't have to."

"Man, if any of my brothers were in this situation? I'd want someone to kick that asshole's ass first, but I'd want someone to be there. You got friends or family in the area?"

Evan squinted, looking like he was thinking. Then, he shook his head. "Parents, one sister, all back in Vermont."

"Long way from home." Josh patted his shoulder. "Did you, uh, live with him?"

Evan scrunched his face up. "Sadly, yeah."

"Ouch. What an asshole."

"Yeah." Evan smiled slowly at him, like he was really seeing him at last. He *was* getting it together, if not sobering up yet. Unfortunately, with that came embarrassment. His gaze dropped to the floor, his cheeks burning bright red. "Sorry about… uh… everything."

"God, stop apologizing," Josh teased lightly.

"Sorr—uhh." Evan pinched himself.

Josh laughed and patted his back. "I'll grab you something. Any dietary restrictions?"

Evan just smiled at him and shook his head.

"Casserole will do you good. Be back in a minute."

Josh spirited away the whiskey bottle—adding more whiskey on top of those four drinks wasn't a good idea.

Back at his place, he packed a couple servings of casserole into a takeaway container. The cabins were equipped with utensils and cookware, so he didn't have to bring much.

It couldn't have been more than ten minutes before Josh came jogging back down the path toward the cabin. He immediately noticed the freshly rinsed-down porch. That saved him a gross job, at least.

The question of how was answered when he saw the ice bucket on the rail, upside-down, dripping.

A problem-solver, Josh approved. At the farm, especially out of sight of tourists, they often made ends meet with solutions that weren't elegant, but worked.

He'd expected something more… obnoxious rich boy about Evan. Especially with what Leo had told him he overheard from Monty. But it was sounding more and more like Monty was just a dick.

That sure as hell fit with Josh's experience of him earlier that day.

He'd wished something better for Evan, but maybe not so

immediately, and not caused in part by him. It was hard not to feel a little guilty.

When Josh knocked lightly and let himself in, he noticed that the interior of the cabin was tidier, too. Evan had cleared off the table of miniatures, put away his luggage, and turned on the lamps.

It looked cozy in here now, and Josh took a moment to admire the place. Each of these cabins was surprisingly expensive to outfit, but he hadn't skimped on the furnishings or decorations like some hoteliers. It had paid off in return visitors and positive reviews.

"Hey." Evan sat at the table now, fidgeting with his phone and spinning it across the surface of the table.

Josh held up the container of casserole. "We'll get this in you and you'll feel better."

"That's what he said." Evan smirked at him.

Josh laughed, letting him have the moment of humor. No doubt he was still feeling embarrassed about all this. He grabbed plates from the kitchen cupboard and heated the casserole up again.

Then, Evan's smile vanished, replaced by a much grumpier pout. "Not that he even wanted *that*, near the end. I shoulda seen it coming."

"Wait, you mean..."

Evan pushed a hand through his hair self-consciously, looking down at the table. "Yeah. I guess I could have put more effort into, I dunno, looking my best..."

It was impossible *not* to notice that Evan was hot. High cheekbones, full lips, perfectly back-combed hair, and those eyes. There was something enchanting about the way Evan watched him.

"Bullshit," Josh shook his head and snorted. "He'd be crazy not to think you're hot."

Evan looked startled enough that Josh could tell he hadn't been fishing for a compliment. And, worse yet, he could tell that he hadn't *gotten* any in a long time.

The more he talked to Evan, the more he wanted to punch Monty in his smug little face. He'd just let something great go, but clearly he'd never deserved him, either.

"Oh. Um. Thanks." Evan was blushing again, staring back at the table. It was impossible for Evan to hide his smile, though.

Josh smiled, too. If he could make the guy feel a little better throughout this shitty moment in his life, that was all he wanted.

He couldn't rescue everyone, as much as he wanted to sweep Evan up and show him how he deserved to be treated.

Besides, now would be the worst possible moment to hit on him. He wasn't a slimeball who'd go around taking advantage of guys in shitty situations like this. Monty probably was.

Josh set plates in front of them both and took a seat opposite him at the little table.

"I really appreciate you being here," Evan told him. "And feeding me. And... I can't thank you enough."

Josh shook his head. "It's the least I can do, like I said. You had a shitty day, and if I can help... well. That's worth it. Dig in."

Evan wolfed down food like he hadn't eaten in days. With those cheekbones, maybe he hadn't. Josh immediately wanted to fatten him up this week. For some reason, he just made Josh want to take care of him. How weird was that?

It wasn't until they were both finished that Evan sat back

again. He still looked like he'd been drinking, but he wasn't blindingly intoxicated now.

"I should let you get to bed, or call your friends and family and stuff," Josh finally spoke up, gathering the dishes and plopping them in the sink.

"You've been… more than good." Evan walked him to the door. The way he hesitated told Josh what he wanted.

Josh opened his arms in an invitation, and Evan took it.

Their bodies were warm and solid together. Evan's breath was warm on his cheek, and his forehead rested naturally on Josh's shoulder.

They hugged for a little too long. It wasn't awkward, though, somehow.

"Take care," Josh murmured and waved.

He left the cabin as quickly as he could and didn't look back. That way, he might not admit to himself that his heart was racing sixty to the dozen.

Wrong time, wrong place. Don't even get ideas.

He couldn't save Evan from dealing with his life explosion. God, he could barely save himself. What right did he have to any more than a thank-you?

Stupid, he told himself, and the voice was his dad's. Reminding him that he was stupid, lazy, and poor—and he was never gonna escape that.

Josh wasn't the kind of rich guy Evan was used to, even if he was nice. Nice didn't pay the bills.

Josh couldn't give Evan the attention he deserved. Hard-working didn't make memories together.

Josh wouldn't make a good boyfriend for anyone—least of all Evan.

It wasn't even worth daydreaming about.

Four

EVAN

Crap, Evan's head hurt.

That's what you get for drinking the mini-fridge, dumbass, he told himself, but the message didn't sink in. The brief oblivion seemed worth it, even right now in the aftermath.

It hadn't just brought relief from anger and desperation and the terror of figuring out what he was gonna do now to make ends meet. He also felt weirdly guilty that he didn't feel worse.

Monty had never been kind, but he'd always been fair. Suddenly flipping his lid and acting like Evan had done nothing for him? That was the weirdest shit he'd ever experienced in their four years together.

What a waste of time.

Evan pushed himself upright, then groaned and covered his face. Light hurt; movement hurt; sound hurt.

And all he wanted was someone—not Monty, but someone who gave a crap.

The gentle knock on the door took a second to catch his attention.

Is that Josh again?

He couldn't lie to himself: his heart lifted at the prospect. Josh had already done more than enough for him—more than anyone could be expected to do—but he was greedy. He wanted more of his time and attention and... well, that caring nature.

Except he was also a little scared of it. He didn't know how to let himself be taken care of.

Evan eased the door open and squinted through the gap at the bright light, and the man standing in it, framed and haloed. Like his fucking guardian angel.

At this rate, maybe Josh was.

"I thought you might want toast." Josh held up a bread loaf.

Despite his headache and queasiness, Evan giggled. There was something about the sight of the broad-shouldered man delicately cradling a loaf of sliced bread in one hand, earnestly looking at him.

Wasn't there a kind of jay that did that? Brought presents to its mate?

Not that he needed to be thinking about mating with Josh. Not a chance. Josh was just being nice to him, and now wasn't the time to take up another fling. He'd been with Monty long enough that he wasn't sure how a fling worked, exactly.

"Thank you," Evan finally managed, stepping backward to let Josh inside. "My head's killing me."

"You got something for it?"

"Yeah, in my medicine... kit... bag..." Evan gestured hopelessly at the bathroom.

"That combo didn't agree with you, did it? Good thing we didn't bust open my whiskey," Josh said and grinned. "Go get pills for your head. I'll make toast."

Evan had thanked Josh so much that he wasn't sure he could do it again. He just nodded slightly and stumbled for the bathroom.

By the time he'd freshened up, Josh had buttered toast ready on plates, and Evan's appetite had slowly started to return. Coffee and toast went a long way to making him feel human enough to be able to talk again.

"Oh, man. I guess I have to sort everything out today."

"Your place to live?" Josh frowned as he brushed his crumbs into his hand and dumped them on the plate.

Evan couldn't clearly remember what he'd told Josh about his living situation or… well, anything. He blushed and nodded. "I lived with the guy for years. God, I probably don't even remember how to sign a lease. I haven't since college."

"What'd you study?"

"Marketing. I was pretty good at my job, and then I quit it to do it for his company…" Evan trailed off, frowning. "Ugh." It was an unpleasant reminder of the trust he'd placed in a man who'd just utterly screwed him over. "But I should have seen it coming."

"I'm sorry, man. He was using you. Doesn't mean you deserved it," Josh told him, stacking the plates. "We've all been there before."

He looked reminiscent, and Evan was curious what was going through his mind. Then, Josh turned on a thousand-watt smile again. "But if you wanna keep busy this week, there's always things going on around the farm."

"Unless I have to go back and apply for jobs in…" Evan trailed off and furrowed his brows. Where exactly were these jobs? Not many in Vermont, and he liked the southern winters better anyway. Hell, he could move anywhere he wanted now.

Josh raised his brows.

"I don't know where I even wanna live," Evan laughed. "Wow. I never thought I'd even be thinking about this."

It was completely surreal: sitting in a rental cabin in a state he'd never been to, talking to an almost total stranger he'd met a day ago—and whose shoes he'd thrown up on. Newly single, unemployed, and unwillingly free.

"Okay," Josh said slowly, stretching and lacing his hands behind his head. "Seems to me you shouldn't rush into anything. I hate to ask, but… it's over, right? You guys aren't the on-again-off-again kind?"

Evan laughed sharply. If Monty came crawling back, he'd have a lot of words for him. "No. Neither of us are."

"Just checking," Josh said with an approving nod. "I won't have to scare him off, then."

The fact that Josh was willing to do that for Evan made him smile. "Nah. I'm not gonna be over him for a long time, I bet, but I'm not going to make the same mistake twice."

"Smart man." Josh laughed under his breath. "Took me a long time to learn that lesson."

Again, Evan wanted to ask, but it seemed too personal. Then again, his life had been splashed all over Josh's front step—a little too literally. He drew a breath to ask.

Then, he lost his nerve.

Josh had been kind as anything to him. He was clearly a caretaker—the kind of guy who made sure his friends were okay, and even strangers. What the hell right did Evan have to ask him about his life?

Instead, he mumbled, "I gotta say it again. I'm sorry I

dragged you into all this. Getting smashed in your cabin, dumping all this emotional crap on you…"

Josh looked thoughtful. "You've been trained to apologize for being human. Don't do that."

"What?" It took Evan a few seconds to even start to process that, but his gut instinct told him *ding ding ding, pay attention to this.* "Er, sorry. What do you mean?"

"I think you know," Josh said slowly. He was searching Evan's face like there was something he wanted to find in it, and Evan felt…

He felt like a deer in the headlights. But not the way Monty had made him feel. That was more like *an insect pinned to a card.* Something for Monty's collection, but not something that was supposed to have its own opinion.

Evan didn't get the feeling Josh was watching him and deciding how he fit into his own plans. Instead, he seemed to be observing.

The attention made Evan blush and look down.

Yeah, he'd apologized to Monty for his feelings enough over the years. He'd always thought he was oversensitive, and Monty the practical one. Monty's opinion always won.

"I guess you're right."

Josh squeezed his shoulder and rose to his feet. "I'm always right. Ty—my best friend—would disagree." He grinned.

Evan smiled back. "I bet." He'd never had someone close enough for long enough that he'd call them a best friend. Not since he'd been in grade school.

Another thing he's got that I don't. But he clearly deserves it. I have to work for it.

"Get a nap. You still look awful," Josh told him.

Evan snorted. "Thanks for the honesty."

"I don't have a lot to offer," Josh said with that stupidly charming grin. "That's the main attraction."

From a glance alone, Evan would have disagreed. He was gorgeous, clearly strong—the muscles under his plain t-shirt rippled—and had charming manners. The kindness he'd shown Evan over the last few days contradicted his claim of not having much to offer, too.

"Don't say that," Evan told him, shaking his head. "I won't believe a word of it."

"You're clearly addled and in need of sleep." Josh grinned and waved as he strode for the door. "Catch you later."

With that, he was gone, and Evan was still staring at the door ten seconds later, willing him to come back through it.

Goddamn. Josh was a mystery he wanted to solve, but this was not the time.

Five

JOSH

END OF SUMMER BROUGHT MORE HEADACHES THAN JOSH could handle every year.

Now, not only was he worrying about activity leaders and cleaning staff, but even his goddamn store staff couldn't bother turning up.

Just as Josh had suspected, Adam hadn't turned up today. Another blue-sky flu had struck. He oughta get his immune system fixed.

Josh sighed and tapped on the counter, swinging himself around and around on the stool behind the counter.

Unlike a lot of hellish employers, Josh let his employees at this little shop sit down on shift. No point in forcing them to do the hard physical labor of standing for hours. They were only supposed to be minding the register and stocking shelves, and it was easier to be cheerful when their feet weren't hurting.

They weren't an authentic Wild West place, either, so phones were allowed so long as they kept them out of sight when customers were around.

He poked at his own phone on the counter, playing a bubble-popping game. Covering this part of the shift himself was boring as hell, but easier than finding someone with half an hour of notice to work these last few hours in the evening. Sometimes he did paperwork, but he'd caught up on most of it not long ago.

Josh scrolled through his group text thread with the guys. Just as he'd told Evan, they'd all met back in high school, bonded before all of them even knew they were gay or bi, and somehow they'd all kept in touch.

"Fancy meeting you here."

Oh, crap. It was Mr. Hottie McSingle himself, looking much more alive than he had that morning. It was all Josh could do to keep himself from blushing as he shoved his phone aside and nodded politely. "Here for supper?"

Evan grinned at him. "I thought I might feed myself, for a change."

"Really? My cooking is that bad?" Josh pretended to pout. "I'm wounded."

"No!" Evan looked like he was about to leap over the counter, his hands held out. "No, dude, I didn't mean that. Your casserole is to die for. I want the recipe." He was rambling now, looking more animated than he had since the breakup.

Breakup, Josh reminded himself. Wrong time to hit on him.

Instead, he just grinned. "Aw, sure." He waved around. "Pick up whatever. You've got credit on your room."

"Really? Another prepaid thing? Sorry I didn't get out today for any activities, by the way. I kind of slept the day away."

That sounded a lot like depression, which he couldn't

blame the guy for, but Josh didn't want it to get a grip on Evan. He hoped his lying face held out as he nodded. "Yeah, all prepaid. No problem, man. Just join in whenever. I'll tell 'em you might. We always have people drop out anyway."

If it would help get him out of the room and socializing with people again, totally worth it.

"I might tomorrow, actually. I'm trying not to think about jobs yet." Evan grabbed a few essentials: Josh tried not to watch, but he noticed a box of mac and cheese, milk and butter, bread, cereal. Enough that the guy wouldn't starve himself. Phew.

They only had the basics in stock—nothing too fancy, but enough for people to use the kitchenette to feed themselves without having to drive into Knoxville to go to the store. Which came in handy since he was pretty sure this ex-couple had come in one car.

"Fucking jobs," Josh agreed. "Hey, if you need a ride wherever, let me know."

"Oh, I couldn't put you out of your way," Evan shook his head. "You've already done so much."

"I could do with some time away from this," Josh admitted and laughed, ringing the purchases up to Evan's cabin number.

"What *are* you doing here, anyway?"

"Covering a shift. A guy was sick today. I suspect he'll be sick tomorrow morning, actually, but..." Josh rolled his eyes. "Not that we know anyone who might get hangovers."

"Shut up," Evan laughed. "And don't restock my mini-bar. I don't need that temptation."

"Wise man." Josh handed back the goods in a bag. "All good?"

"I guess so."

Josh wanted to invite him over, but however fragile the boundaries between them were right now, it felt like that would be a fatal blow. And if he let his guard down a little bit...

Evan might just sweep it all away, and then he'd leave and nothing would be the same. Or worse, Monty would get his claws into him again.

"Dirty Dancing is on tonight." He said it before he even thought, and then blushed. Fuck. That was the least graceful way he could possibly ask him over.

Evan furrowed his brow and gazed questioningly at him.

Josh shut his mouth before he said anything that might get him into trouble, like *Come on over and we'll watch chick flicks and get drunk together.* That wouldn't look at all like he was trying to get in Evan's pants.

"Is it? I'll scroll through the channel guide and see," Evan grinned. "I guess it's a fitting movie for... here," he gestured around. "Are there dance classes?"

"We have had line dancing here," Josh laughed. "And swing."

"No way." Evan laughed. "Speaking of stuff I never..." he trailed off, then rolled his eyes apologetically. "Sorry. This will turn into Monty-bashing fast."

Josh grinned. "I'm down with that. The guy dumped you during your engagement photo shoot—planned it ahead of time by trying to check out early—and took off, leaving you literally stranded in Tennessee. Did you live in New York City?"

"Yeah," Evan admitted, his cheeks flushing as he looked down.

"Shiiit." Josh winced. "That's a long way from home. Yeah. Dick."

Evan shrugged. "He always was, I guess. I'm only realizing that now."

"Better late than never. You dodged a bullet, man."

The shop door rattled and Josh jumped. Somehow, talking with Evan had distracted him. He'd nearly forgotten they weren't alone at the farm. There were, of course, other guests.

"Mrs. Elliot. Hello," he greeted.

Evan raised a hand and ducked toward the door, much to Josh's disappointment.. "I'd better take care of supper. Are you—I mean, did you wanna… I should return the favor."

Josh blinked a couple times, and then smiled. "You don't have to, but if you want the company…"

"Yeah. Yes, if you want." Evan clutched the bag close to his chest, fidgeting with the plastic handles. "Cool. Sweet. What time…?" he trailed off.

Josh checked his phone. "Gimme forty minutes."

It wasn't a date. Nothing even close to it. He was just hanging out with a new buddy and helping him get past a tough spot in his life.

So why did Evan give him that excited, yet shy smile? And why did his heart race when he looked after Evan? And why was it so hard to tear his attention away from Evan and look back at his next customer?

Getting involved with Evan would be a terrible idea. Way too many reasons not to do it. Perfectly good reasons: the conflict of interest if he was also giving Evan a place to stay; the freshness of the breakup for Evan; the fact he'd only be a rebound.

None of that stopped him wanting to get to know Evan— more about who he was and what he cared about, what made him happy and what he was going to do with his life now. He wanted to help and rescue Evan, but even beyond that, he wanted to uplift him and watch him fly. Something in Evan called Josh to pay attention.

Josh was playing with fire, and he knew it. But he was tired of playing it safe, too.

It was just mac and cheese and a movie. It wasn't even Netflix and chill.

Don't you dare take advantage of him, he told himself as he made idle conversation about Mrs. Elliot's day on the farm. From the sounds of it, Monty had spent years doing just that. He wasn't gonna be one more dick in Evan's life.

He was going to be a friend to Evan, and make sure Evan had what he needed to heal.

That was all.

CHAPTER

Six

EVAN

It had been a long time since Evan had been propositioned. Now that he thought about it, nearly as long as he and Monty had been together. He'd been putting all the hard work into their sex life—pun totally intended.

Had Monty really just been using him for his company branding? If so… fuck him.

He was essentially a smarmy kid with rich parents, trying to leverage that into being a lifestyle influencer on Instagram. He dabbled in tech investments, partied on yachts, and designed fashion.

The closer Evan looked at it, the less Monty actually did himself. He had people to tell him who to invest in. He took up other people's invitations and graced them with his presence (especially if they had expensive champagne), but never bothered organizing his own events unless he'd get something out of it. He partnered with designers, putting his name on their work.

It was more complicated than that, but that was what his

business boiled down to: exploiting others with a work ethic or anything he wanted.

Why the hell hadn't Evan seen that earlier? He'd believed Monty's stories about wanting to connect with people and connect them, leverage and build engagement, all that marketing bullshit to describe what was essentially... a non-job.

If Monty's "company" disappeared tomorrow, who the hell would notice? He could go on partying, and people would go on doing what they did before him, and nobody would lose.

Evan gritted his teeth as he checked the clock again. He was determined not to start the mac and cheese too early, or it would be cold by the time Josh came over.

God, he didn't know what he'd do without Josh. He still hadn't called his family or friends—not that he had many of either. Everyone expected him to be off the grid, on a fancy romantic retreat with Monty. They were all excitedly waiting for the engagement photos.

His parents would be pissed off and upset. His sister would threaten to string Monty up by the balls. His few friends—the couple people who had ever paid attention to him back in Vermont, before he rubbed elbows with the social elite of America—would want to drive down here and rescue him.

And he wasn't sure he deserved to be rescued from this trap of his own making. Moreover, he wasn't sure he *wanted* to be.

Finally, the clock ticked from 7:34 to 7:35 PM, and he let himself start making dinner. He'd always timed dinner to be ready exactly when Monty was home from "work," but this felt different.

Cooking supper gave his hands something to do to keep busy, at least. That calmed his thoughts down, and they drifted away from his dickhead ex.

It felt less terrifying to consider what he was going to do now… more like an open sky of possibility.

Maybe it was these very open skies and the fresh ranch air giving him a chance to breathe, to think. He couldn't imagine the kind of black hole he might have gotten sucked into if Monty had dumped him in the same kind of way that he'd proposed—in the heart of Manhattan—and driven home without him.

Vermont didn't feel like the right place to go back to. His parents and sister lived there, sure. He got along with them fine, but he couldn't live there. New York was out, except upstate—somewhere quiet, rural.

But with August fading into September, summer would be packing up and going home very soon in the northern states. He didn't have strong ties anywhere else.

I wish I could just stay here. From what little he'd seen of Knoxville as he'd directed Monty to a gas station, then out to the ranch, he'd liked it. All the charm of the south, vibrant, and bustling. Friendly people—from his sample size of about five people—and a pretty nice climate.

Above all else, it was beautiful here. He could look across fields of wildflowers to the mountains, distinctly set against low clouds and alluring in the near distance. Knoxville lay in the other direction, warm and welcoming.

He could see why Josh had chosen this spot.

There was a knock on the door, just on time. When he opened it, Josh stood there.

Evan had spent years registering, cataloging, and judging by appearances. He couldn't fail to notice that Josh had changed into a nicer collared shirt and clean, dark jeans. Like he was on a date.

"Honey, I'm home." Josh smirked at him.

Evan stuck out his tongue and let him in. "You're always at home here on the ranch. I was just thinking that. About how lucky you are, living in a place like this."

Josh grinned. "You could be, too."

"Huh. I was thinking that, too. But I dunno. I'm putting off that thought until tomorrow," Evan admitted, laughing.

"That's a good call. Just keep unwinding," Josh agreed.

The nervous tension between them was impossible to miss, and totally new. Before, it had been completely cool between them. No stress, no expectations. One broken man and one man trying to help him hold the pieces together.

Now, though? It was like they saw each other afresh, but with that extra vulnerability that came from their last few days together.

"Macaroni's ready," Evan said, gesturing at the table. He'd set it with the basic tableware supplied at the cabin: placemats, coasters, glasses of water.

"Still no booze?"

Evan chuckled. "Hell, no. I wanted a clear head tonight." He didn't add, *So if I hit on you, I don't have any excuses.*

He didn't need to. Josh caught his gaze and held it, then slowly smiled. "Wise man."

"I can be."

Evan served up the bowls of mac and cheese. "Sorry it's not much..." he started, and then Josh's words came back to him. *I'm apologizing for being human. I shouldn't. I'm sharing what I have, and what I can get a hold of here.*

"Thank you. It looks good," Josh answered. He even

seemed to mind his manners as he carefully picked up his fork.

This was the weirdest date ever.

They both polished off their bowls in record time, making casual chit-chat about their days. Evan didn't have much more to say about his, having spent the day in bed, but Josh was animated.

"Fucking kids who don't know how to work a day in their lives. I mean, I've been dealing with this guy all summer. Covering shifts when he can't be bothered to show up. Monday mornings when he's obviously hungover. It's getting real old."

Evan nodded sympathetically as he pushed his bowl back and stretched. "I worked a couple campus jobs when I was in school. A lot of people were like that. Not just kids, either."

Josh sighed. "No, you're right. There's people twice my age who can't be bothered to stop playing Facebook games long enough to actually manage the reception. I don't mind people not giving a hundred percent. It happens to all of us. I'm the owner, I have the most stake in this place. But at least put *some* effort in."

"Ugh. Laziness is my biggest turn-off. I can't believe I let Monty—sorry," Evan added, laughing. "He's like the punching bag right now."

"Good." Josh grinned at him. "Punch away."

"He was lazy as hell. He was good at looking like he worked hard, but that's not the same." Evan sat up straighter as it came to him. "There's people who make hard work look easy, like you. And I respect that more."

Josh blushed and waved a hand. "Oh, well," he dismissed it.

"All that and humble," Evan added, smirking as Josh's blush deepened. "And you blush easily."

Josh rolled his eyes at him. "We'll miss the start of the movie if we're not careful." He moved to the bed, sitting on the edge like he didn't quite belong there.

"Oh, right," Evan said, laughing. As Josh turned on the TV, he drew a breath to steady his nerves. "I kind of figured it wasn't about the movie anyway." He had no idea how to ask the question without coming right out. Or was that what one was supposed to in the dating world now? Even a few years made a big difference. Hell, he'd never been on Grindr.

The way Josh eyed him, he knew what he meant.

"Netflix and chill?" Evan grinned. He followed Josh to the bed, taking the longer route to climb onto the other side of the bed. "Or did I, like, totally misread this—"

"No," Josh cut him off, laughing. "Nah, you didn't." Thank God Evan wasn't the only one who'd noticed. His pleasure at Josh's answer was short-lived, though. "But I can't take advantage of you."

Okay, that was ridiculously chivalrous or an elaborate excuse. Evan eyed Josh to figure out which it was. "Really?"

"As far as I can see, you're out of a home, job, and fiancé all at once. If I slept with you now, it'd look like… like…"

"Like you were helping me get out of a hell of a drought." Evan grinned. Josh was being entirely too sweet to him, and it wasn't anything close to what he wanted.

He wanted to feel good. He wanted to forget Monty's touch—or rather, since Monty hardly touched him, he wanted to be touched by someone who gave a crap.

"Drought?" Josh frowned. "But it's been, like, two days."

Evan scowled. "You know how long it's been since he bothered helping me get off? Sure, if I bugged him, he'd *let* me do him favors. And the last time we fucked? I don't think he stopped watching TV the whole time."

He'd never told people this. Hell, he hadn't had people to tell. He sure as hell couldn't talk to his family, and his friends in Vermont weren't really that close. Any friends he'd made in the city were friends of Monty's, not his.

"Oh, Jesus." Josh looked pissed. "You deserve better than that, man. But I don't know if I can be the one."

"I don't want you to be *the one*," Evan told him. He reached across the queen-sized bed until he covered Josh's hand with his own. "I want something to help me forget him. I *want* a rebound."

He'd never been this kind of guy before. Never slept with a guy to get over another guy, never dated a guy without first planning who would take whose surname. When marriage was legalized, his fantasies had come that much closer to reality.

And then Monty had taken and taken and never given back.

Josh was spoiling him, and he knew it was greedy, but he wanted more. Couldn't stop himself wondering what it would be like to be spread out on the bed under those kind, strong hands. Couldn't resist fantasizing about Josh's arms wrapped around his waist, hoisting him up against a wall or onto the desk as he fucked him slowly.

God, the years of sexual frustration were unwinding all at once. He was getting hard at just the thought of Josh touching him, and the warmth of his fingers on the back of Josh's hand.

Even was pretty sure he'd only last about thirty seconds, but goddamn, it would make up for the last five years.

"Please," Evan added in a whisper. His cheeks burned as

he looked down at the comforter. "If you don't want me that way, it's fine. But don't make me the reason you say no."

Josh's voice was hoarse. "Are you sure? It's been a while since I broke up with anyone, but I remember how… intense it is."

"I'm goddamn certain." Evan took Josh's hand and dragged it across the bed until it rested on his hard cock. He snuck a peek up through his lashes at him.

Josh looked startled, but so turned on. He was breathing heavily, and as Evan watched, he licked his lips and swallowed hard. Even the sight of his Adam's apple bobbing made Evan horny.

He knew it was a stupid idea. He was probably throwing away a perfectly good friendship. If Josh couldn't look him in the eye again after this, he'd kick himself for years to come.

But Evan also knew that if he let Josh walk out of the cabin without so much as a kiss, he would regret it for the rest of his life.

"I wanna feel good tonight. That's it. You don't have to marry me," Evan laughed. Josh grinned back at him, and Evan's heart soared. Josh's hand still rested on his hard-on, and he wasn't pulling away. The response had him feeling hopeful again. "You've done so much for me. I can't ask for more, but if you want a night of fun… we both win."

"Yeah." Josh pulled his hand back, but before disappointment gripped Evan, he crawled toward him on the bed. When he lay next to him, Josh ran his hand up Evan's thigh again, all the way to his stomach.

God, even that one touch was blissful. Evan shivered, already tuning out the movie in the background. He squirmed against Josh's hand, sinking back against the pillows.

Josh propped himself up on his elbow, lying on his side next to Evan. His hand still wandered up his chest, all the way to his cheek.

"I thought you were hot the moment I saw you. I was kind of pissed off that you were taken by such an asshole," Josh admitted with a quiet laugh. "It felt like… too good to be true. I mean, not for you," he hastily added, cupping Evan's cheek.

Evan laughed. "No. It's good for me, too. I'm… free. To do whatever. *Be* whatever."

The thought hit him—or maybe he hit *it*—like a brick wall. *But all I wanted was to be loved.*

Then, Josh's lips were on his, and Evan gasped into his mouth. Warm, soft, and gentle. Josh's stubble scraped his cheek as he turned his head at an angle, and Evan grabbed his shoulders to pull him in even closer.

He couldn't decide if his heart was heavy or light. The realization was a kind of grief—for what he should have had, and the years he'd spent chasing it—but also excitement.

Evan *could* find more. Maybe not with Josh. Maybe Josh was just a way to a better future. Or maybe there was something here.

For once, Evan didn't want to over-plan it. He just wanted to go with the flow and see where this took him.

And right now, it was taking him to a blissful paradise with just the two of them. Josh's kisses were gentle but constant, lending him a kind of reassurance and strength. Evan hardly remembered how to respond at first, but his body and instinct took over.

He pulled at Josh until Josh straddled him, then ran his hands gently up his back to lace in the back of his hair. The kisses grew deeper, more frantic now. Wet lips slid on lips, and Josh's teeth caught his lower lip. The way he kissed—his tongue dancing along Evan's sensitive skin until Evan gasped —was absolutely intoxicating.

I never realized how much I needed this.

Already, Evan felt sexier than he had in years. Wheedling and coaxing like Monty was doing him a favor, when it was Monty who wound up receiving all the favors? Yeah, that was part of what Josh had said about him being trained to apologize for being human.

Well, he wasn't going to apologize for this. Not for having needs, and not for wanting Josh to be the one to meet them.

He could feel Josh getting hard against him, and it was a thrill.

The chemistry between them had been muted for the first day, but it was impossible to ignore now. There was something about the way they moved together, like they could already anticipate each other's actions and reactions.

Evan had never experienced that before.

"Yes," Evan gasped when Josh ran his hands up under his shirt, slowly pushing his t-shirt up and off. They had to stop kissing for a few seconds to manage it, and the moment the shirt was free, they went at it again like they'd had years apart.

Even a light touch of Josh's hands on his bare chest made Evan writhe and cry out.

"Shit, you're sensitive," Josh whispered. "I love it."

Evan was blushing—arousal or embarrassment? He wasn't sure. "Monty used to say I was hard to turn on."

"I disagree." Josh's finger flicked his nipple gently, and Evan nearly lost his mind.

The surge of pleasure that rushed through him, head to

toe, sure agreed with Josh's assessment. "Oh, fuck," Evan gasped. "Fuck, that's good."

Josh did it again, then circled his finger around the nub, dancing across it in light brushes.

He leaned down, catching the other in his mouth, and Evan whimpered Josh's name. Josh sucked harder, and Evan could swear Josh's mouth was on his cock, not his chest.

"Josh, I'm gonna come in my pants if you keep that up." Evan arched off the bed, grinding against Josh's thigh.

"Can't have that," Josh chuckled, kissing his way up Evan's neck to his lips. As soon as he could, Evan leaned down to kiss him hard.

Josh fumbled with their clothes, and Evan twisted and squirmed to let Josh pull down his pants. At least he had a week's worth of clothes with him. How he'd get the rest of his stuff back…

No, don't think about that yet.

"Oh, fuck," Evan gasped, jolted back to his thoughts by Josh's hand rolling a condom down his sensitive shaft.

And then Josh *really* blew his mind, via his dick.

The wet heat that closed around him made him shiver. "Oh, my God. Josh." He didn't need to say it—it had been way too long.

Josh swallowed his whole cock, his fingers running along Evan's stomach and curling around his hip. When he pulled his head up and off, he lapped the shaft and whispered, "Good?"

"The way to a man's heart," Evan gasped, giving a breathless laugh as he curled his toes into the bed.

The way Josh used the tip of his tongue to tease Evan, running it around the head and across the slit, made him squirm. But every time he tried to push his hips up, silently begging Josh for more, Josh kept him flat on the bed.

He was taking his sweet time, and goddamn if Evan didn't love it. He was happier than he could remember being in... way too long.

Josh's fingertips ran slowly from his hip up his stomach to his nipple again, and Evan choked on his gasp. It took all he had to hold back, not to embarrass himself as the firm pressure of Josh's tongue did wonders for him.

His skin was nearly burning with pleasure at every touch of Josh's hand. Every tweak and brush of a finger across his nipples sent electric jolts through him, head to toe.

"Josh," Evan panted when the heat and pressure were almost unbearable. "I'm gonna come too fast."

Josh grinned when he pulled his mouth off Evan, teasing his balls with a finger. "If you like this, we got a week."

Like that, Evan's spirits soared. A week with this man? "Fuck, yes." He didn't have to think twice before answering.

And the delicious orgasm that hit him a minute later, pouring through him in all its sweet relief, sure did a lot to lift his spirits, too.

Josh kept gently bobbing his head for a few more moments before he pulled away, grinning up at him. "I love the way you squirm around when you're turned on."

Nobody had ever said *that* to him before. Evan blushed fiercely and cleared his throat, beckoning with a finger for Josh to come up the bed.

Josh settled on his side next to him, one strong hand closing around his rock-hard shaft.

"Oh, I could watch that all day," Evan whispered. When he tried to give Josh a hand, Josh gently pushed his hand back against his stomach.

"Just relax."

Evan took the chance to run his hand up Josh's stomach and chest, over his shoulder. God, he was built. Real farm work did miracles, apparently. This body wasn't just for showing off, but boy, did Evan like looking at it anyway.

Josh's breathing hitched when Evan's palm ran over his nipples, and Evan grinned. "Now I can return the favor."

The little nub stiffened between his fingers as he tweaked it gently, then ran his fingertip around the pink skin.

Josh groaned when he did so, one strong hand closing around Evan's shoulder. His nails bit in, and Evan shivered with delight.

Try as he might to avoid it, he couldn't help but compare. It felt incredible to turn a man on so easily. Evan felt sexier than he had in a long time.

"God, you're hot," Josh whispered, his gaze wandering up and down Evan's body as he jerked himself off, his breath hot on Evan's neck. "I'd do you all night."

"I might hold you to that," Evan warned, winking at him.

Josh moaned. "Please do!"

"Come on me," Evan whispered, wriggling until Josh straddled him again.

"You like seeing that?" Josh's grip on Evan was tight and his breathing quick. "Oh, God. Even the thought of fucking you... yes!"

Evan found himself a lot stickier very quickly, and he couldn't stop grinning. He rubbed Josh's back and side as the contentment settled into his bones. "I'm so glad I hit you up."

Josh flopped next to him and laughed breathlessly, glancing over toward the movie. "And the best is yet to come."

Evan glanced at him, then scooted off the bed to head to the bathroom. "Hope so." His chest was tight with emotion.

A rebound was supposed to be simple and easy and good, wasn't it? Well, this felt good, and it had been easy enough to let go of his inhibitions. But what the hell did this mean for him?

Surely it wasn't a big deal. Like he'd told Josh, it was just sex. Messing around with a guy to get past his hangups.

Well, in some ways it had worked. As he wiped himself clean and brushed his teeth, he dragged his heels deliberately on rejoining Josh. He couldn't decide if he wanted to ask him to stay or not.

When he cracked the door and rejoined Josh, he had his jeans back on but his shirt was still off. He had his arm behind his head, the remote in his hand. Josh glanced over, scanning his face before smiling. "You doing fine?"

Evan nodded. He didn't know how to put into words the tangled knot of emotions. It felt good as hell to be appreciated and desired, and it was surprising and delightful not to have to do all the hard work, for once. But at the same time, he was a little pissed off.

How hadn't he seen it earlier—everything that was missing? Why had he let Monty use him for so long? How dare Monty use him, for that matter?

The bittersweet sensation that flooded him made him scoot toward Josh on the bed when he rejoined him.

Josh pulled him in, wrapping an arm around his shoulders. "They're about to have sex. We beat 'em."

Evan laughed. Settling against Josh's side felt strangely natural—like he'd known him for so much longer.

He closed his eyes for just a few moments. The next time

he opened them, the covers were tucked over him, the light off in the room.

Josh wasn't there.

Evan pulled a pillow close to his chest and hugged it, closing his eyes once more to fall back into sleep.

CHAPTER
Seven

JOSH

It was a weird feeling to wake up alone, with such a vivid memory of warm skin on his own.

Josh sighed as he rolled over in bed and pulled a pillow over his face.

He was usually quick to get up, eager to get to work. The sooner he started working in the morning, the sooner he could wrap up at night. Or at least, that was what he told himself. The work always seemed to expand to fill every available moment of his time.

God, he had to take a break and go out this Friday with his brothers.

He rolled over again, grabbing his phone to check their group text thread and send a quick message.

Hey guys—we on this Fri?

It didn't take long to get an answer, even at this hour. Some of his brothers wouldn't be up yet, but others were early risers.

Oscar was the first to text back. The dancer was up with the sun. *Roman's working late that day but I'll be there.*

One by one, the other guys chimed in. From the sounds of it, about six or seven of them could make it, which was a pretty good turnout.

Then he got a text from Tyler, who was probably his best friend in the group.

Call me?

Sure, he could put off starting his day for a few more minutes. Josh dialed Tyler and sat up, leaning over enough to tug his blinds open. At least it looked like another warm, dry day. No providing ponchos and rain gear to tourists out for trail rides who had been too foolish to bring their own.

"Hey, man," Tyler greeted.

Josh cleared his throat. "Hey."

"Rough night?"

"Just woke up." Josh rubbed his eyes.

"This late? Jesus. Someone keep you up all night?"

Josh snorted. "Not *all* night. Just the first part."

"Oooh. Are you back on Grindr, then?"

Josh wasn't sure he wanted to admit to it, but then again, why not? Tyler would tease the crap out of him, but he might have good advice. "No. A guy—a guest. He got… aw, man. I'll sound like a jerk if I say it."

"A guest? Did you give him a five-finger-and-pretty-lips discount?"

Josh scoffed. "Shut up." That hit a little close to home. He'd spent a good half-hour before sleep last night reminding himself that he wasn't taking advantage of the guy —hell, he hadn't even told him that he'd sneakily given him the week in the cabin for free. There couldn't be any expectations if he kept that fact from Evan.

"Oh, shit. Tell me."

Josh sighed. "Long story or short?"

"Long!" Tyler encouraged him. "I got a couple hours. And I won't make it out on Friday, so I need the details now." As far as Josh knew, he was getting ready for a race that weekend.

"Fine," Josh chuckled. "Guy got dumped by his fiancé in the middle of a wedding shoot—Leo mentioned that, right?"

"Yeah, I saw that somewhere in the group chat." Then, Tyler sucked his breath in. "Oh, *shit*."

"I wasn't planning it," Josh hurried to explain. "But after the dickhead left, I made sure he'd have the cabin for the week so he can get his life back together. He lived with the guy, worked for him…"

"Oh, man. So he just had a triple blow, huh?"

"Exactly." Josh growled under his breath. "If I could find that Monty asshole, I'd do more than reverse that refund."

"Does he know you're hot for him? This other guy?"

"Uh. We kinda slept together last night."

Tyler whistled and laughed. "Jesus, you move fast."

"Don't tell the others yet. On pain of death. Or at least some serious titty twisters."

"I promise," Tyler told him. "So what are you gonna do?"

"What do you mean?"

"Is he dating material, or what?"

That was the part that really bothered Josh. He'd have to see Evan safely home somehow, and then… well, long-distance wasn't his thing. He could barely keep up with a real-life, in-person relationship with anyone further away than Knoxville.

"Well," Josh drawled, trying to get his thoughts straight. "He seems like a cool guy. Definitely my type. Sweet, smart, the whole package. That asshole ex didn't know what he had, really. But his family's up in Vermont."

"Ohhh." Tyler paused for a few moments. "Huh. That's rough. So he's not a local?"

"Not even close. But I guess he'll go where he gets another job," Josh said, trying to reconcile himself to the idea. It had only been a couple days—why the hell did he want to wrap his arms around Evan and keep him safe from the hurricane that had hit his life?

"If you really like the guy, long-distance is a thing," Tyler said.

"You and Alec have a hard enough time being apart for a week, ten days, at a time," Josh reminded him. The cute little doctor had been treating Tyler after his accident a couple months ago, and one thing had led to another.

Tyler's career as a pro driver kept him on the road ten months a year, and he couldn't just drop it.

It was kind of the opposite problem for Josh. He couldn't just walk away from the farm, especially during summers.

"So, can you help him find a job in the area?"

The idea made him blink. "What do you mean?"

"Knoxville, dumbass. Even Nashville. Lots of jobs going, depending—what's he work as?"

"Uh… marketing," Josh answered, his brows furrowing.

"Hey, you're always saying you want more business. Why not ask him?"

It was a weird idea, but hey… it might be worth asking. "The ranch is a little below his pay grade," Josh laughed. "He was at some bigwig New York firm. That's all I know."

"Did he tell you that?"

"I Googled him," Josh admitted in a mutter.

Tyler snickered. "You never know. It's worth bringing up. Even if he does it long-distance, you can keep in contact…"

Josh furrowed his brows. "Look who's become Mr. Cupid."

"Love would suit you, too," Tyler said teasingly.

Josh groaned and rubbed his eyes, swinging his legs out of bed. He had too much to do to be lying around chatting about his crush like he was back in high school. "Fuck off. I gotta get going. Thanks for the talk."

"Keep me posted on Hotty McCuteface."

"Fine, you asshole." Josh laughed. "Good luck today."

Once he'd hung up, Josh took a moment to think about the idea. It wasn't bad, necessarily. It just sounded ridiculous. *I know you're used to big, fancy companies, but what about helping one stupid little dude ranch get more business?*

Plus, his family was all far away. Any friends he had, too. Why the hell would he move all the way to Tennessee just because Josh offered him some stupid little job? He didn't even have enough marketing work to keep the guy busy full-time, and offering him work on the ranch sounded even more ridiculous.

Historically, getting his hopes up had never paid off. It was dumb to start now. But if he grabbed a moment alone with Evan again today…

Maybe he'd ask. Maybe.

CHAPTER

Eight

EVAN

"OH MY GOD, MY THIGHS ARE KILLING ME." EVAN RUBBED them carefully, almost doubling over as he leaned on the fence.

Julio, the instructor, was clearly trying not to laugh at the expression on his face. "You'll get used to it if you keep it up."

Evan eyed his horse and shook his head. She hadn't thrown him, but she'd wandered off-course a little more than he was comfortable with. She'd always caught up to the group again, but it was embarrassing. "No more mares for me."

"You should see Bucky here," Julio chuckled, patting his horse's flank gently. "He's always a handful. I don't think our guests will ever get on him."

"You mean I got an easy horse?" Evan shook his head. He was bowlegged as hell. Oh, God. This was why cowboys looked bowlegged, wasn't it? Would his legs correct themselves again this week, or was he destined to swagger around like John Wayne, only at a gentle hobble?

"Ahoy." That was a cheery and all too familiar voice. Evan

sighed and turned to shield his eyes from the sun. Sure enough, Josh was approaching with a cheery grin, thumbs in his pockets. "How'd our newbies do?"

"I think we could hire 'em," Julio said with a good-natured grin, but Evan suspected he said that every time.

Josh chit-chatted with each guest, asking them about the experience and swapping stories. It was sure something to see him at work, bonding with people and making them feel special, even if he was clearly getting around to talking with everyone.

Surely it was a good sign that he talked to everyone else first, right? After all, Evan reminded himself, he hadn't paid for this. Or had Monty already done so? Josh had been kind of fuzzy on the details, but he was gonna have to ask. He couldn't afford to suddenly have to pay anything if he was about to have to find a job.

And it would be the worst insult to not be able to pay Josh after all he'd done for him. The potential embarrassment made him shrivel up inside.

"Hey there," Josh greeted with an easy smile, leaning on the fence. "He put you on Mona, huh?"

"Yeah, she has a mind of her own."

"Gentle as anything, though?" Josh said with a questioning frown.

Evan shook his head. "Oh, no. She sure is. But she wanders off and... grazes. She just ignored me when I wanted to catch up with the group."

Julio laughed. "Can't stop her when her favorite grass is right there, and a lot more interesting than the rest of us. But she'd never let you get lost. That's why I put you on her." He was leading horses into the barn now, most of them trotting eagerly. Their supper must have been waiting.

"Oh, sure. Put the city boy on the dependable old mare," Evan laughed. "I'm sure she's the widest."

Josh blinked at him.

"My legs are gonna fall off." Evan was still leaning on the fence, and when he tried to stagger upright, his legs told him off for it. "Oof. Ow."

"Oh, no," Josh laughed richly. "You've never ridden before, huh?"

"I didn't even know I had muscles there!" Evan protested. "Oh, Jesus."

"Tell you what. I've got a hot tub on my back deck. After this, I gotta check in with reception, but then I'm free. Soak the ache away, or you'll be stuck in bed tomorrow," Josh told him.

Evan's heart skipped a beat. Was that an invitation? He sure hoped so. "Uh, sure."

He didn't have a swimsuit—hadn't expected there to be any swimming opportunities out here. Maybe he ought to give Josh a heads-up.

Since Julio was busy with the horses, Evan leaned in and murmured, "Don't have a swimsuit. Is that a problem?"

Josh smirked at him. "I don't mind a sausage boil. Or I can give you a lift to town to get something..."

That sounded like way too much effort to avoid something Evan kind of wanted to do. "Are you joining me? Isn't a party if it's just one."

"I'd be delighted to," Josh told him. "I'll even scrounge up something for supper. Come on up at five. You know where mine is?"

"It's the house up there, right?" He'd noticed a larger place, set further back from the cabins and somewhat hidden by the trees.

"Sure is. Don't pass out before then," Josh warned with a laugh.

Evan grinned. ""I'll try and stay awake somehow. Grab a shower and be up later, then."

"See you." Josh made it sound like a promise, not just a statement.

"See you soon." It took all Evan had to brush past Josh and head for the gate back to the main road, and up to his cabin. All he wanted to do was grab Josh's hand and tug him back to the cabin.

God, the sex had been great. If he was in for more, he'd keep his hands to himself in the shower.

Tempting as it was to let his mind wander back, he somehow managed to get himself clean enough for the hot tub, and chose his loosest shirt and shorts to pull back on afterward.

He felt so underdressed. At the bottom of his bag sat his usual clothing—dark suit pieces, now-wrinkled dress shirts, ties. Two changes of clothes, in case they headed out to a fancy restaurant on the spur of the moment. That was Monty's habit, after all.

But now he was stuck here, without a home, car, job, or fiancé, and he couldn't remember the last time he'd smiled so much.

Was this all a dream?

He knew one thing for certain: if he woke up tomorrow and Monty were at his side, he'd kick the fucker out of bed faster than Monty could call him *needy*.

Evan let the door bang open as he headed up to Josh's house, darkly shaking his head. "Needy, my ass."

"I can help there."

The shock made Evan slip on the stairs, missing a step.

The adrenaline rushed to his head, but before he could do more than gasp, he was in a strong, familiar pair of arms.

"How the hell are you always there?" he gasped. He wasn't pulling back from Josh, though. He liked being nestled against his body, especially with the thrill that had shot straight to his dick from the rush of tripping over his own feet.

"I'm your personal stalker. And, apparently, bodyguard." Josh shook his head. "Didn't mean to startle you. I apologize."

Evan finally, reluctantly, pulled away from that musky scent and the warm touch of Josh's hand on his back. "I'll let you get away with it. Only 'cause you're handsome."

"Oh. I'll take a compliment from your pretty lips."

Somehow, Josh had turned the tables on him. How the hell did he do that? And why did Evan love it so much?

He knew he was turning bright red from the way Josh grinned at him.

"Th-Thanks?"

"Now, about this hot tub."

As he followed Josh up the trail, Evan shook his head. He wasn't just sticking around for the fresh country air. He had to be honest and admit that to himself.

But Josh couldn't be more than a rebound, either. Not with the timing and circumstances in which they'd met.

But he also didn't want him to be just a rebound.

But wasn't that the definition of a rebound?

Sadly, his minibar was still out of stock, but it was probably for the better. Alcohol wasn't going to help him find that clarity.

God, he was screwed.

"Come right through. Or inside. Or on... I didn't think through my pickup line." Josh held the door open for him and grinned. "Did it work anyway?"

Evan laughed. "You can blame me for startling it out of you. By falling into your arms."

"Oh, I feel so lucky. It's not often a gorgeous guy falls into my arms."

"You don't run around scaring the hell out of them?" Evan shut the door behind himself and stepped inside, glancing around at the place.

Josh grinned. "I don't, and they don't run around telling me their ass is empty, or something like that..."

"Needy, I said!" Evan flushed before he even finished the sentence. Wait, that wasn't the important thing to clarify. "I mean—"

Josh snickered. "Oh, it's needy. Sorry. Same difference, ain't it?"

"I'm beginning to think you're hitting on me, Josh." Evan shook his head. "Nice place here, by the way."

"Thanks." Josh gestured around. "A few rough spots I've always planned on getting around to finishing, but never really did."

Evan couldn't tell. It all looked rustic to him, compared to the fancy Manhattan penthouses he was accustomed to, but he wasn't going to say that and sound like a total asshole. Instead, he just smiled. "It's very... I don't know. Homey."

"Could be cozier," Josh said with an easy shrug and smile. "But it's good enough for a bachelor."

Evan was struck by the image of Josh wrapped up in the comfortable throws that lay on the back of the couch, all alone in front of the fireplace this winter. Meanwhile, he'd be somewhere closer to home—New Jersey? New York, upstate? Connecticut? In front of an electric radiator in a crappy little place, spending his days at some soulless agency and working his way to the top again.

Christ, that was a sad thought. Where had that come from? He was supposed to try to be happy now, wasn't he?

Evan shook his head. "Good enough for sure. So, where's this mythical hot tub?"

"Right this way, sir," Josh teased. As he walked through the place, past a huge kitchen island to a patio door, Evan shadowed him, putting a hand in his lower back.

Josh looked startled but slowed down and smiled at him sideways. "How you doing, anyway?" he asked, with surprising insight into Evan's shift of mood.

"It's weird," Evan admitted. "Still doesn't feel real. In both a good and bad way."

The hot tub was already full, and Josh dipped a hand in. "Should be good for us to climb in now." He fiddled with dials, and jets came on. "Want a beer or anything? Aw, hell. I should offer you wine and be fancy about it, but I'm not sure what I have. Red? White? It's all pretty crappy."

He was acting nervous now, talking fast. And Evan suddenly noticed that he was rubbing at his neck.

"What's the matter? You know I'm not picky."

"I just…" Josh trailed off, then sighed and pulled his shirt off, carefully folding it as he kept his eyes on what he was doing. "This must all seem real backwoods to you, you know?"

"It does, a bit." Evan had a new policy about honesty. He didn't like lying, and he didn't like being lied to. He'd sniffed out some of Monty's lies before, but he hadn't seen through him to the rest nearly quickly enough. "But that's not a bad thing. It's just different. And hell, I was never really comfortable with Monty's life. I'm still an outsider here, but people aren't judging me for not knowing which fork to use. So I'll have whatever you're having."

Josh nodded and clapped his shoulder. "Back in a minute."

While he was gone, Evan took a glance around. Only trees and fields as far as he could see. There weren't huge privacy fences or concierge desks, but you could strip buck-naked and no one would see—or probably care.

It was a different kind of freedom than the financial freedom Monty had given him, which came with social restrictions.

But this couldn't last, so he'd better enjoy it now.

He sighed as he stripped down and slid into the hot tub. God, the water beating against his aching muscles was indescribably good. By the time he'd adjusted to the temperature enough to climb all the way into the water, Josh was back outside, carrying a beer can in each hand.

"Thanks," Evan said with a grin, cracking it open and clinking it against Josh's. Then, he had the pleasure of watching Josh strip.

He was already shirtless, his shoulders broad and muscles defined all the way to the waist of his jeans. A dusting of hair crept up to his navel, and as Josh dropped his jeans, Evan shivered with pleasure. The same fine, blond hair he'd felt last time lightly covered his thighs and shins, too.

And his cock, softer than the last time he'd seen it, looked delicious. Evan hoped he had a chance to taste it this time.

Josh climbed into the tub, giving Evan an even better view. He didn't even try to hide his stare as he grinned up at him. "So, if we've only got a week, do I get to play with you this time?" Evan teased.

"Actually," Josh said, "I was hoping for something... else."

"I'm down for anything, in or out of the tub." Evan smirked when Josh blushed. "Any way you want me—"

"I mean, would you work for me?"

Evan couldn't wrap his head around that. "I'll ride, sure. Not just gonna lie there and let you do the hard work—"

"Nooo," Josh groaned, laughing. He pressed his beer can against his cheeks as if they were hot.

Evan was feeling the burn himself. Sweat trickled down the back of his neck. Though his muscles still ached, it was a dull throb instead of the fiery regrets that had taken him immediately after dismounting.

It wasn't actually too dissimilar to riding a guy, which brought his brain right back to that distraction, and it took a few seconds for him to register what Josh was saying.

"Work *for* me. As in, I could employ you. I know you've got better offers, and not so far away from your family. And I can only promise work until Christmas, at this rate. But if you want, I always need someone reliable. It's not glamorous, either. A bit of marketing, but also a lot of odd jobs, physical work, pinch-hitting—"

"Yeah." Evan smiled when Josh looked startled. "It sounds perfect."

Josh lit up. "Really?"

That giddy expression made Evan smile, and forestalled his concerns before he could even give voice to them. This wasn't some pity job offer, and it wasn't a joke.

Josh had complained that it was hard to find decent help around here. And Evan was in need of a job. There was one small issue, though.

"Can I find a place nearby?"

"Well…" Josh lifted himself out of the tub to sit on the edge, his beer loosely gripped between his fingers as he rolled the can around in his hands. Evan tried not to get distracted by the direction of the water trickling down Josh's body. "That's the thing. I have a guest room. I don't know how comfortable you are with, you know… sharing space."

Evan stared up at Josh, his mouth hanging open. He was practically a guardian angel, wasn't he? "I—I can't—would you…" he stuttered, then mirrored Josh to sit on the opposite corner of the hot tub and cool off.

"I have friends stay sometimes. I've had 'em around for a couple months before. If you want a place to stay while you find your feet—and there's no point in signing a lease if you're gonna take off to, like, New England…" Josh shrugged. "It's only practical."

"I'm beginning to think you have a heart of gold under that gruff country boy image," Evan teased. He wished the light would fade earlier in the evenings. It was hard to hide how overwhelming the invitation was for him.

Josh snorted and waved a hand. "I hide it well."

Oh, man. I have to take the offer, don't I? Evan dug his fingernails into the can and traced them around, etching circles in it. "Why are you giving me so many chances?"

"Chances?" Josh shook his head. "You just happen to need things that I've got. A spare room, a job." He shrugged.

"A dick?" Evan grinned.

Josh hesitated. Whatever was on his mind, he didn't want to say it, so Evan stayed silent until Josh finally had to answer. "I don't think that's a good idea." When Evan widened his eyes and pouted at Josh, he laughed and held up a hand. "Oh, don't give me those eyes. They're dangerous."

Evan grinned. "Are they?" He let his smile drop after a moment. "So, why not?"

"Conflict of interest. Employer and employee."

Evan had had a feeling that was coming, but he hadn't prepared an argument to counter it. So he just nodded, tapping his can against his knee. "Four more days of fooling around with you, or four months of working for you."

"Suppose it's an easy choice," Josh said, but the words hung between them like a test.

Evan smiled to himself. *I'm going to make this work somehow,* he promised himself. *I have to.* "I wouldn't go that far, but it's a logical one." At this very moment, Evan wanted to slide around the side of the hot tub and join Josh.

It was impossible not to notice the sweat droplets trickling down his chest and stomach. As Josh languidly swished his feet through the water, his cock shifted against his thigh.

God, Evan was horny again.

"Don't suppose we could wait to make it official until the end of the week? So I can have my cake and eat it, too?" Evan tried his best pleading eyes.

Josh licked his lips. "We'll sign the contract Monday. I think that would be best. You need time and space to get..." he trailed off. "Get your life on track," he finished half-heartedly.

"Get over my ex. You can say it. I know." Evan laughed to himself. What was there to get over, besides a potential lifetime of self-esteem issues?

Josh chuckled. "I wasn't gonna rub it in."

"That's very considerate." Evan scooted around the edge of the hot tub rim. Then he yelped, "Whoa!"

His bare ass slid over a wet spot on the edge 'rend he slipped in, like it was a goddamn water park slide. There was a tug on his hand, but he was too far gone.

Evan choked on the swirling jet of hot water and pushed himself up with his hands against the seat until he stood up and was clear of the water. He spluttered and coughed, rubbing his eyes. "Jesus!"

Josh was laughing his ass off—and where the hell was his beer? Josh had one in each hand. "Starting to think you might be clumsy, man."

"You asshole," Evan laughed. "You saved my beer and not me?"

Josh held it out to him. "Are you sorry? You get a beer, I don't have to shut off the hot tub."

"And I get a dunking!" Evan took the beer but reached out to pinch Josh's nipple.

Josh yelped and laughed, squirming away. "Sorry, sorry. Next time I'll put a non-slip coating on there."

Evan winced at the thought of that grinding against his ass—or worse, his balls. "Oh, Jesus. No."

"That's what I thought." Josh's eyes sparkled as he wrapped his arm around Evan's shoulders. It was a loose, friendly hold—enough to indicate interest, but not so tight Evan couldn't brush the arm away.

Evan didn't. He reached up to lace the fingers of his free hand with Josh's, closing his eyes for a few moments. "Bet this is nice in the winter."

"Oh, you have no idea." Even when it was quiet, Josh's voice was husky and warm, easily audible from this close distance over the jets of the hot tub.

"I might find out, though?" Evan stared across the valley and rolling fields, watching daylight gradually dim. Twilight was a couple hours away still, but the late afternoon glow was distinctly a fall afternoon.

This place would be so easy to fall in love with.

"The offer stands." Josh sounded nervous. "If you don't

want to, that's completely fine. Obviously. I mean, it's just an offer. And it's not much."

"It's… the time and space I need to get through this. It's helping me restart my life." Evan shook his head. "It's *not* not much."

Josh hummed. "I dunno. I reserve the right to be an asshole later."

"And I might be some lazy, money-grubbing jerk." As he said it, Evan's heart sank. It wasn't what Monty had said word-for-word, but it was the spirit for sure.

He didn't think of himself that way. But was he? Josh was offering him all this stuff…

"No," Josh said firmly, his hold on Evan tightening. "He said shit to you because he was pissed off about whatever his own internal world is. That don't matter. *He* ain't in charge here. I'm offering you a hand up, not a cozy life. It'll be hard work. Dirty, sweaty work some days. But you aren't flinching from that."

Evan shook his head, forced to admit that Josh was right. "No. That's not what bothers me. I just feel like… I should find my own feet in life."

Josh let that one stand between them for a few moments as he kicked his feet in the water. "I can see that prideful streak in you. We've all got one. Pride is stupid, though. Pride gets you broke—hurt—even dead. Pride never did shit for anyone, when push comes to shove."

"Cheerful." Evan chuckled and leaned into Josh. The warm weight of him was solid and reassuring, as was the way Josh reacted by protectively sliding his hand further down Evan's chest. "But yes. I accept. And… thanks."

The word wasn't adequate—it felt like he'd hit rock bottom, but he'd bounced off it already. He was just clinging to the edge of the cliff, but Josh was helping. Josh anticipated his needs before he even realized he had them.

Josh grinned. "But true. One more soak before we head in? I'll find something for supper."

Evan let him change the subject, but Josh's words stayed with him as they soaked away the stresses of the day, then hurried between the hot tub and the house.

It was warm enough that they didn't need to run, but chasing Josh inside gave him an even better view than he'd had from the hot tub.

"Gotcha!" He tagged Josh just before Josh managed to get the door open.

Josh turned and grinned, then grabbed the back of his head to haul him in for a long kiss. His lips slid across Evan's —seeking, finding, claiming.

When he pulled back, Josh breathed out, "You sure do." Then, he turned and headed inside, grabbing a towel from a shelf near the door and tossing it at Evan.

Still dizzy from the sudden and intensely passionate kiss, Evan only just caught the towel before his boner did.

He could get used to being kissed like that.

CHAPTER

Nine

JOSH

"THAT *THING* YOU DO WITH YOUR TONGUE."

Josh lay flat on his back on the living room floor, covering his face with his arm as he tried to catch his breath.

Evan's smirk was obvious even from his tone of voice. "What thing?"

"You know perfectly well what thing," Josh said, sliding his arm away from his eyes and grinning at him. "In fact, I'd argue you're playing innocent."

"I don't need to play innocent when you like me being filthy."

Crap. Evan had him there. Josh stuck out his tongue. "I sure do, gorgeous."

He'd gotten more action in the last couple days than he had in weeks—maybe months. Apparently Evan had been serious about wanting to get as much sex in as possible before he started working for him.

Josh glanced down at his stomach, still streaked with Evan's load and his own sweat. "I'm gonna need another shower," he laughed. He'd been getting out the door later each day, but since he'd always been one of the first up and around, nobody had noticed.

Or if they hadn't, they didn't dare say anything.

It was Friday, and he had no idea how he was gonna explain this to his brothers, but he wanted Evan to come along. If he was going to be here for a few months, it just made sense.

But Josh was also keenly aware that every time one of them had introduced another guy to the group, they'd wound up dating—or engaged—within a year. No wonder Tyler was disappointed to miss the chance to make fun of him.

No way could it work out, though. As far as he knew, none of the other guys had met under these kind of circumstances.

As Josh headed to the bathroom to clean up, he faced reality.

He was just a rebound—something better than Monty. And he was happy to be that guy for Evan. Swapping blowjobs and messing around for a few days instead of a one-time-only event didn't change that.

"Got any plans today?" he asked Evan, buttoning up his shirt for the second time that morning as he headed back to the living room.

"I thought I might walk around the place and learn the ropes a little better. Maybe introduce myself, if you're all right with that." Evan was sprawled across the floor, sitting up against the edge of the couch.

God, Evan was pretty. The sight caught Josh's eye for a moment: the slender, strong form, graceful even now. Those dark eyes always felt like they penetrated him to his core.

It made Josh feel uncomfortably exposed, like Evan knew every one of his secrets.

That was stupid and Josh knew it, but the way Evan watched him wasn't just a careful inspection. He seemed genuinely interested in everything Josh did, and that made a nice change. Not like a hookup who was here to fuck and fuck off.

"That—that's fine," Josh stuttered, trying to pull his thoughts together again. It was promising that Evan wanted to get a head start on the new job. "Just let 'em know you're the new general help."

"Will do." Evan pushed himself upright and leaned in to press his lips on Josh's for a second, then headed for the bathroom.

Backing off on Monday was going to be the hardest damn thing he'd done. If only weekends weren't his busiest time.

Now that Evan had moved in—which just meant helping him move his luggage up to the farm house, and handing the keys in to reception for cleaning—it was gonna be even harder to resist.

But, for now, he had ranch business to deal with. He couldn't afford distractions—quite literally.

—-

"I want a refund. This is unacceptable!"

Josh's stress levels were creeping higher by the second. The guy by the desk was being obnoxious and not even listening. "And as I said, sir, you can't wait until checkout of a seven-day vacation to say you're not sleeping well."

The brazen things people would do to try to save money. He bet this guy was the type to go to a restaurant, eat everything, and then complain that it hadn't been cooked properly to try to get a refund.

Practically speaking, he couldn't afford to refund someone for an entire week just to keep them quiet. And morally, he couldn't justify it. Why should someone be able to lie and rip him off, when decent people had to pay up?

Not a chance, man. Josh didn't fold his arms, even when the other guy did, but he stood firm.

"I'm gonna tell all my friends and family about this ripoff joint. I'll leave you a Trip Advisor review and warn everyone!"

Bad reviews were the usual threat people turned to these days.

"Good thing I'm not offering a refund, then," Josh said mildly. "I can't offer any monetary incentive to change your review. That's against the rules."

The guy spluttered and turned red, then flipped him off. "Fuck you, and all your useless fucking staff. My lawyer will be getting in touch!"

"I look forward to reading the case he builds," Josh answered, still smiling. Killing 'em with kindness was the best way he'd figured to deal with customers like this. He couldn't and wouldn't be drawn into an argument.

But after the guy stomped out, the adrenaline finally hit, and he found himself shaking. His throat went tight, his eyes stinging.

It was far from the first time and wouldn't be the last time he reacted like this. He did what he always did—turned and headed for the office, shutting the door firmly behind himself.

Everyone knew that when he did this, they should leave him alone for an hour or two. They could sort out their own crises, and if anything too drastic happened, call the office phone.

Josh settled at the chair behind the desk and closed his eyes, taking deep breaths.

The office hadn't changed much since the days when it had been a real ranch.

All the cabins were new—added by him, when he took over the ranch a few years ago after his dad's death. But this had been one of the original buildings. It was still his dad's desk in here, and photos lined the office walls.

The building was steeped in the history of the ranch, and its most recent owners. It dated back to the 1890s, though the building itself had burned down in a fire a few decades later. It had been largely rebuilt, but very well. It still stood here, solid and imposing.

And here he sat, figuring out how to make it work as a tourist attraction, hollowing out the actual ranch activities to make room for clueless city folk. God, Dad would have hated it.

Then again, Dad wouldn't have approved of much about him.

Josh rocked back in his chair and put his feet on the desk. It didn't matter, he reminded himself. This place was *his* now, free and clear and outright.

No mortgage to pay on the ranch or land. Only the loan for the renovations, and he'd been steadily paying it off over the last few years.

When all costs were paid, it didn't make him a lot of extra money yet. He had good seasons and bad ones, and he had to bank up in case of the latter. But this was also his cost of living mostly covered, so he didn't need much.

And hard work made him happy, whatever Dad used to say.

Josh sat up straight and pulled piles of paper toward

himself. He needed to catch up on his accounts. The peak summer season was just about over now, and he was staring at empty cabins throughout the autumn.

He had to do the math on whether he'd be better letting them sit empty or dropping his price on a booking site to try to attract more business.

Even the best season of the year had passed without much fanfare this year. He'd been busy enough, sure, but not as busy as last year or the year before. And he had no idea if that was down to any decisions he'd made, random chance, his ratings online, or what. Could just be a travel industry change.

He'd hoped to avoid the headache of farm management, in an effort to avoid becoming his dad—easy to anger, quick to the bottle, and slow to help or praise people around him. Instead, he'd traded it for a whole new industry.

His accountant was visiting tomorrow, and he'd wanted to pull together his documents, but he would have rather been outside mucking out stalls or cutting grass or fixing a window.

Anything but sitting behind a desk, wondering if his business would make it out of the deadly first-five-years window of entrepreneurship.

Sooner he started, sooner he could quit work for the day and drown his worries in a hot tub and a can of beer. And maybe Evan's pretty eyes.

The temptation was there to use Evan to escape his stress, but that was probably exactly what Monty had done. Evan deserved better.

Like a guy who knew what he was doing around a farm, or one who didn't run away when the going got tough. Or one who didn't freak out at one raised voice. God, what kind of man was Josh, anyway?

He grumbled under his breath and leaned over to switch on the coffee maker, then ripped open a handful of envelopes. Time to deal with this shit so he could get outside and play in the autumn sunshine.

Winter would come, like it or not, and he, the business, and the ranch all had to be ready.

CHAPTER

Ten

EVAN

EVAN NEARLY JUMPED WHEN JOSH STUCK HIS HEAD AROUND the corner of the kitchen. "Boo."

"Shit! I didn't hear you get home," Evan laughed. "I was thinking of cooking."

He'd just spent the last few minutes wandering around, pulling open cupboards and trying to figure out what he could make.

The advantage of the kitchenette in his cabin was that he could only cook simple foods—things he couldn't screw up. With well-stocked cupboards and a full kitchen, he had no excuses for fucking up supper.

Josh eyed him. "Orrr," he drawled, "we could go out for supper."

"That'd be awesome." Evan didn't care if he had to put it on a credit card. He'd rather eat out and figure it out later than embarrass himself trying to feed Josh some terrible meal.

He'd done just fine feeding himself and Monty, but then, they'd eaten out for many of their meals anyway, or Monty would eat at work and come home full. Josh, though? He deserved the best. Evan wanted to impress him.

Stop comparing, he told himself. *Just because he seems better in every way doesn't mean anything. We're not doing the same thing. This isn't dating.*

"Wanna come out tonight and meet some of my buddies? I guess I should have started with that," Josh laughed. "I usually take a taxi in, eat supper, meet up with the guys for a few hours, drink a lot, head back here."

Evan laughed, but his heart skipped a beat. Monty hadn't introduced him to friends for the first four months. "Sure," he said casually.

"Great," Josh nodded. "I'll let them know to expect you. They're all good guys. Fun to hang out with. You might have to deal with wedding planning, though. Deen is in full-on Groomzilla mode."

Evan laughed as he closed the cupboards he'd left open and checked his pockets for his wallet and phone.

As Josh grabbed his keys, he paused and looked at Evan, then pulled open the drawer of a stand by the door. When he pulled out a single key, Evan already knew what was coming.

It stung just as much as it thrilled him: he had a key to another man's house, and he'd barely moved out of the last guy's place. But again, he reminded himself, it wasn't the same. *More's the pity*, he added mentally. Josh would make a hell of a boyfriend.

But no, he was gonna be a hell of a boss, and he'd already been a hell of a friend. Evan didn't deserve more.

"Here's a key to the place, in case you wanna come back early or anything. And it makes sense."

"Yep," Evan agreed briskly, trying to keep it as professional and lowkey as Josh was doing. "Makes sense." He took the key and turned it over in his hand, then pocketed it. He was gonna have to get his keychain from his bag later and swap the keys out.

That was a weird feeling.

Josh squinted at his phone. "Uber's just about here. It's hit and miss whether they wanna pick people up this far out of town, but it's easier than talking to taxi dispatchers," he chuckled.

Glad for the distraction, Evan nodded. He trailed after Josh to the parking lot. He'd spent the day doing laundry. He'd sorted out the luggage, wadding up Monty's stuff into a messy heap before tossing it back into the suitcase. His own things were now neatly folded in drawers and hung up in the closet of the guest room.

Being a dickhead's cool...

Music played from very close by, just as they reached the parking lot. The lyrics were familiar to him, but it took him a moment to recognize that it was his own phone going off.

"Oh, shit." Evan scowled as he answered the phone. It was their first contact in nearly a week now. He must have been drunk when he changed that ringtone. "Hey, Monty."

The only thing that kept his blood pressure from boiling was that Josh started to laugh, barely stifling the sound behind his hand.

"Hey. I thought I'd check in." Monty didn't sound angry or brusque like he had last week, but the silence since then spoke volumes.

"Right. A week after leaving me in Tennessee," Evan laughed. "Sure. What do you want?"

"Well, I was going to offer help with your living expenses while you get a new place."

That sounded awfully generous. Evan raised an eyebrow. "Why?"

"Doesn't really matter, does it?" Monty asked. "If you want, so you can get an address and I can get your stuff back to you."

That didn't sound right. Evan scratched his head as he thought. "Right... but no. I'm fine. I've got a new job and a place to live."

"Oh, good for you." Evan knew that tone well. Monty was keeping his distance, acting like he didn't care. And for all Evan had been able to tell, he really didn't. He never hung up and went into a fit of anger, or paced, or anything. He just shut off like a goddamn machine.

He resisted the urge to be snarky. "Yep."

"And," Monty continued, bringing them to the point he'd suspected was lying in wait. "I talked to my lawyer. He wants you to sign some documents."

"About what?" Evan didn't know a lot, but he did know not to sign anything without looking it over with a lawyer present. Monty's legal team had drilled that into him. He idly wondered which lawyer it was. "Which lawyer?"

Was it Brown, whom he'd served lunch to last month? Taylor, whose house he'd been to for dinner? Miller, who had gone to some ribald off-Broadway show with them?

"Thompson."

Evan should have known. Slimy bastard wouldn't know friendship if it bit him in the ass. Maybe he'd planted the idea in Monty's head that Evan was being a drain on him.

"Right," Evan said tightly. "Thompson wants me to sign away my paternal rights?" Humor deflected the emotion of the moment. He'd been dumped in the middle of what was supposed to be one of his happiest moments, and now he was signing away his rights?

Josh smiled at him in a reassuring way. Evan leaned into him, and Josh wrapped his arm around Evan's shoulders.

"He thinks it's best if we formally sever business ties. The contract just says you're giving up all rights to the branding and marketing campaigns you created for the business."

That was cold, but it explained Monty's attitude. This was all business.

Evan grimaced. "Yeah. I don't want any of it anyway. Send it over and I'll sign it on my phone or whatever." At this point, he would have been happy to walk away from all traces of his old life. This was the perfect way.

"Excellent." Monty sounded like he'd just negotiated some "collaborative" co-branded vision session or some crap like that.

There was a moment's pause. Evan wondered if Monty was thinking how goddamn strange it was to talk to each other like this.

"So, that's a no on the money?"

Evan snorted. "Are you trying to pay your conscience off?" Josh's hand tightened on his shoulder and he saw the Uber pulling up. This wasn't exactly the kind of conversation he wanted to continue in the Uber, so he immediately added, "I mean, that's a no."

"Glad to straighten that out," Monty said, as if he'd said nothing at all. "I'll have my lawyer email you the contract." Again, *my lawyer*, not using his goddamn name, even though Evan knew him.

"Fine," Evan said, his voice clipped. "It'll be sent back by Monday."

"Great."

Monty disconnected, just like that.

They knew each other better than almost anyone on Earth, after three years of living together, another year dating before that, and friendship first. But even now, the inside of Monty's head was a goddamn mystery.

Josh let go of his shoulders and stepped forward to make the necessary small talk with the Uber driver, while Evan tried to put his thoughts in order again.

It was strange how fiery his anger toward Monty was, but also the icy numbness of his emotions after that talk.

Guess it'll take a while for me to get over him, like I said.

Josh scooted in first and buckled up. When they pulled away, he looked over at Evan. "Ready, set, fire."

"Oh, it's not much. He just wants me to sign some goddamn contract to give up the rights to any ideas I brought to his company."

"Seriously?" Josh's jaw dropped, and he looked dumbstruck. "He called a lawyer?" God, he was sweet and naive if he thought that wasn't standard practice for rich people's relationships.

Evan smiled. "Just like an employee."

"Really? Cause, to me, that just seems like a dick power play."

"No, that was when he offered me money." Evan shook his head and patted his hair into place.

His hairspray was just about empty. Full-sized toiletries were his first stop, but he had to get out to a store first.

He'd given up his car last year to commute on the train when he did need to go to the office, and he wished he hadn't now. God. He'd need a cheap beater.

"Money to... fuck off? Hush money?" Josh asked, looking concerned.

"He'd never be crude enough to put it that way, but sure. If you like." Evan offered him a crooked smile. "I'm guessing you've never had an ex who was this much of a dick."

"Guessing right." Josh shook his head. "It just doesn't seem right."

"Lots of people do ugly things to each other just because they broke up." Evan touched the back of Josh's hand. "I never knew if it was because they were fundamentally bitter assholes, or if they were good people who didn't know how to express their anger and grief."

Josh blinked at him a few times and then laughed. "You're processing all of this like a star. In your shoes I'd just be calling my friends up to key his car."

"Would you really?" Evan grinned.

Josh went sober for a moment and looked away, out the window. "Suppose not." Strangely, though Evan had meant it as a compliment to Josh's good nature, Josh seemed to be taking it a little differently.

"So, Monday?" Josh prompted.

"Huh?"

"Is that what the contract deadline is?"

"Yeah," Evan said. "I dunno what happens if I don't sign, but I don't care. If one document gets him out of my life for good, I call that a win."

"I call it a bullet narrowly dodged." Josh mimed dodging one, for good measure.

"God. So narrowly it whistled past my ear," Evan said and laughed. "I can't believe it. How close was I to doing something so stupid?"

This time, it was Josh who took his hand. "I don't think you're stupid at all. You counted on him and he let you down. That just makes you… trusting."

Evan grinned at him. "Which a lot of people would call stupid."

"I'll let the point go for now, but don't consider this argument over." Josh wagged a finger as they reached downtown Knoxville. "I'll bring you back here in the daytime so you can sightsee. Have you been before?"

"Never," Evan said. "We drove through to get gas and then headed to the ranch." He leaned away from Josh now, looking out the window at the passing clubs and restaurants. Nothing like the nightlife he'd been used to, but there was something far more personal already.

"Just at the corner here," Josh told the Uber driver. "Thanks, man."

Evan eyed Josh when he led him toward what looked like a dingy little dive bar. "You come here a lot?"

"And, despite appearances, I haven't gotten food poisoning yet," Josh promised him.

Evan missed the handy hygiene grade sticker that New York places had to display, but he was willing to take Josh's word for it. "Okay. Let's see what Knoxville has to offer."

CHAPTER
Eleven

EVAN

As it turned out, Knoxville had delicious burgers to offer.

Evan moaned his appreciation as he wolfed down the gourmet burger—but not *too* gourmet, like the ridiculous ramen-bun burgers or charcoal burgers. Just a few nice toppings, some perfectly cooked meat, and tasty buns.

"Knoxville has some tasty buns."

Josh smirked. "I'll second that. You should see when we get to the dive bar where we all meet up. It's not a gay place, but a lot of us wind up there."

"And make it gay by your presence?" Evan nodded. "I approve of this motion. And any tasty buns."

"What motion? The back-and-forth—" Josh started, and cracked up when Evan rolled his eyes. "My sense of humor never grew up. Sorry."

Evan coughed and took a swig of his pop, then shook his head as he finished the last bite of his burger. "I appreciate it, but without warning…" He saw the look on Josh's face and laughed. *"Don't."*

"I didn't say a word. That was all your dirty mind." Josh held up his hands and smiled, which was a strangely innocent look considering what Evan knew about him.

"My mind isn't—oh, lord. How will I survive these next few months?" Evan pretended to seek advice from the ceiling, rolling his head back.

"I'll try to be less, uh…"

"Less you?" Evan shook his head. "No way." The jokes might have been unsophisticated, but that was why he liked them.

Monty never would have deigned to make them. Sex was an off-the-record, almost an under-the-covers, affair for him. Except when Evan pushed him to try something different, which made Evan feel pushy and needy.

But with Josh? It was natural, and relaxed, and fun.

"Do we really have to stop what we're doing on Monday?" he asked. God, he never would have had this conversation without preplanning and preauthorization from Monty.

Josh finished his drink and leaned back, looking thoughtful. "I think so. I mean, I trust my ability to be a hardass if you turn out to be a shitty employee."

"Oh, good." Evan laughed. "I'd hate to get away with anything I shouldn't."

"But it's other employees that are the problem," Josh said. "Are you willing to deal with the hazing and the jealousy and the backstabbing?"

Evan stared at him. "You make it sound like a free-for-all."

"It's not that bad, honestly. Some of the people there, I've known or worked with for years. They won't care. And nobody will care about the gay thing. They know I am."

"But?"

"It's more the young guys, or the seasonal workers, or the

ones who wouldn't know work if it bit them in the ass. If you're a hard worker *and* you sleep with me... well, I can't promote you or keep you on but not them. Not without them crying wolf."

"Right. So it'd make your life easier," Evan said. That was reason enough for him to avoid enticing Josh into some long-term friends-with-benefits arrangement.

"Plus, it's probably good for you to have some time figuring out who you are and what you want these days." Josh signaled the waiter for the check and handed over his credit card.

Evan wrinkled his nose. "I'd rather not think too much about any of that. But yeah, I guess you're right."

"Of course I'm right. I'm always right." Josh signed the slip when it was brought back, thanked the waiter, and led Evan outside.

The nervous anticipation of meeting Josh's friends for the first time was only growing.

"Here we are!" Josh pointed out the bar.

Evan swallowed hard. "Cool."

Josh glanced at him, then clapped his shoulder. "They'll like you. No stressing out."

"I barely met Monty's friends until we'd dated for..." Evan trailed off, then flushed with embarrassment. "Not that we're dating."

Josh's eyes sparkled with amusement. "Any time you want to compare me to that dick, go ahead."

As he tried to overcome his moment of vulnerability, of so nearly admitting what he really wanted, Evan winked. "Just between us, yours is a lot more satisfying."

"Oh, is it?" Josh's chest swelled, and Evan hid his smile. That moment of egotism was a strangely adorable look on him.

He strode into the bar, but instead of leading Evan in, he kept him by his side. Evan only realized when they were approaching the table that he wasn't used to this. He was used to just falling in behind.

Christ. So many subtle differences.

"Hey, guys!" Josh beamed at everyone. God, there were a lot of people here. Evan suddenly felt self-conscious, but he tried to tamp down the anxiety. "This is Evan."

Oh, there was Leo! He recognized one person, at least.

Of course, that person was the guy who'd seen his engagement implode in the space of an hour.

Not your fault, Evan reminded himself and smiled at Leo. "Hi."

Suddenly it made sense: how had Josh known to come find him? Leo must have told him something had happened.

Leo rose to his feet to hug Evan and kiss his cheek. "Hi, hon. How's it going?"

"Oh, you know." Evan smiled as he hugged Leo, then settled in a chair between him and Josh. "Still disoriented by everything."

"I don't blame you." Leo pointed around the table. "This is my boyfriend, Dustin. That's Nico and Deen. Oscar—Roman's at work. Falcon—same with Blane. Tyler's away, and… anyone know about Alec?"

"He's supposed to be on the way," Falcon said, leaning in to answer the question. "He was being all shy at first. I had to twist his arm to come."

"Ugh, all these guys with their day jobs keeping them busy," Josh shook his head.

Evan stared at them as the names washed over him and he tried to cling to them, connecting each to the matching face. Thankfully he had practice being on Monty's arm, meeting people he'd later find out were important in some way or another. "This isn't even all of you?"

"Nope!" Josh grinned. "We rarely manage to get us all together. It's pretty random luck when we can get the whole clique together."

Evan laughed and shook his head. "I've never had a clique." God, he hoped this wasn't some high school clique, though. The only groups of gay friends he'd had—through Monty—tended to be full of drama as everyone dated or slept with everyone else. Except Evan, of course, but he'd had his suspicions about Monty.

"You do now. First rule of Gay Clique: we wear pink on Wednesdays." Deen winked. Evan liked him already.

"Will you be around next week?" Dustin asked. He was soft-spoken compared to the others, it was already obvious. "We were thinking of a movie outing. We haven't done a lot besides hang out and drink lately."

Evan nodded, looking back at Josh. "He's given me a place to live and a job, so… I'll be in the area until at least Christmas."

"For a few months?" Nico looked curious.

"Yeah." Evan cleared his throat. Come to think of it, he hadn't asked Josh why the time restriction. Was it a financial thing? Or personal? He couldn't very well ask now, though. "I don't know any of my plans yet. I'm new here. Uh, I don't know if Leo mentioned my story…"

Leo looked sheepish. "I might have. I couldn't believe what that asshole did to you." There was a sudden clamor of agreement among the other guys, who nodded or shook their heads and scowled.

The support left Evan breathless for a moment. "I—" He

resisted the urge to defend Monty. "I, uh. Thanks, guys. I mean, it's for the best."

"Oh, you dodged a real winner with that one." Josh glowered at his drink. Before he could rant about Monty, yet another man walking up to the table caught his eye. "Alec! You made it!"

Greeting him distracted the guys from feeling sorry for Evan, which was a bonus. Then Nico headed off to get a round of drinks, and Alec held out a hand. "I'm Alec. Are you a boyfriend I haven't met yet?"

The snickers and not-so-whispered *yes*es around the table made Evan blush. "No," he insisted firmly as he shook hands. "I'm a friend of Josh's. I was a guest on his ranch, and… er, life happened. So he invited me to stay and work."

There was no way of putting it that didn't make him feel like he was mooching.

"Oh!" Alec smiled at him. "That's great for you both."

"He starts on Monday, and he's already done more to help than half my summer help," Josh interjected, rolling his eyes.

"Is that kid at the store still giving you attitude?"

"Yeah." Josh scoffed. "Like he owns the fuckin' place. Kids, man."

"Hey, we all had attitudes like that when we were eighteen, nineteen."

Nico chuckled as he returned with a round of beers. "I dunno who we're talking about, but boot camp beat that out of me."

"Me too." Leo's lip quirked into a teasing smile.

"Oh, shit, man." Nico laughed. "Not to disrespect *your* boot camp."

"I dunno if NASA went easier than the military," Dustin chuckled. "You barely talked to us for a couple months."

Evan felt lost, but he tried to keep up. Nico had been in NASA? Leo in the military? He suddenly felt like even more of an underperformer.

Thankfully, perhaps sensing his discomfort, Falcon interjected. "So, have you seen much of Knoxville yet? Or has he kept you chained up on that farm?" The grins and snickers were even more obvious this time. Falcon rolled his eyes at them, but joined in the laughter. "Sorry, these guys have the maturity of a bunch of kids…"

"Now I see where Josh gets it." Evan grinned. "It's a refreshing change. I'm used to stuffy boardrooms and business dinners. Ugh."

"You're from the east coast, then?" Oscar asked.

Evan chuckled. "How did you guess?"

"The west and south doesn't do that stuffy self-importance crap." Oscar leaned back and nodded. "Trust me. I was in professional dance. I've toured every state. But Tennessee is home."

"You all sound like you're from the south, though. As far as I can tell," Evan quickly amended. "I don't know if I can move here and… you know… fit in."

"Oh, sweetheart, don't you worry." Oscar leaned over to pat his arm. "People 'round here are nice, but we're not fake-nice. If we don't like you, we'll let you know. Back in New York, New Jersey, Connecticut… guys would say one thing to your face and another to your back."

"There's people like that everywhere," Alec argued.

"That's a good point." Oscar looked around the table at the others. "We're not, but some guys are."

"Can't escape the drama even here," Evan lamented. But he already felt comfortable around these guys, and he could see why Josh had stuck with them. "You've all known each other for a while, yeah?"

"Since high school. Josh, your turn to tell the story," Leo said and grinned.

Evan raised his eyebrow, wondering what he was about to hear, but it turned out to be simple and kind of cute.

"We all went to a high school dance without girls, because… well, some of us are bi, but we're all into dudes and none of us were dating chicks at that point. They tried not to let us in without significant others so we couldn't accidentally spread our gay over their nice little dance. So we were like, *what about significant brothers?*, and then the name kind of stuck." Josh shrugged and swigged his beer.

"That's…" Evan laughed. He could see Josh pulling it off, too. Sounding polite, yet sending a firm message that he was not going to pretend to be someone else for anyone else's sake. God, he admired that about him. "Wow."

"And then we've added some boyfriends and fiancés to the group," Leo added, grinning. "In fact, Josh is the last single guy."

No wonder everyone had reacted like they did to Evan's presence. He instantly felt even worse about leading them on. He couldn't be that last guy to complete the group. God, no. Josh deserved better than a pushover who was on the rebound and mooching off him.

"I'm married to my business," Josh grumbled. "It's more expensive than a husband anyway."

Nico mumbled into his drink, "You say that…"

"Hey!" Deen smacked his arm as everyone laughed. "I'm making this wedding as small as I can."

Leo snorted. "Says the rock star."

Evan did a double-take. "Okay, is everyone here... like... famous?"

Though Josh grinned, it wasn't a mean or teasing look. He put his arm around Evan's shoulders. "Sorry, man. I should have explained better. Deen *is* a rock star. Nico was an astronaut and now he works for the Park Service. Forest ranger," he added. "Falcon's an artist. Oscar was a dancer, and now he runs a dance studio. Dustin's a forensic... something forensic-y."

"Oh, my God. I can tell them a hundred times and they'll never remember." Dustin sighed and drowned his sorrows in his beer.

"Forensic nerd. That's the one." Josh smirked when Dustin flipped him off, and continued. "Leo—well, you know he's a photographer now. He was a... photojournalist?" When Leo nodded, Josh added, "With the military. And then Alec's a PT, fixing up sports guys."

"Right." Evan was blushing again. "I'm a ranch hand these days."

Josh elbowed him. "Don't sell yourself short. What did you do before?"

"Do I have to tell the class?" Evan laughed.

"He's a marketing wizard," Josh stubbornly told the rest of the group, and Evan found himself subconsciously reacting to the pride in Josh's voice. His chest swelled a little, and he sat straighter. "He helped his asshole ex build some big company."

"Oh, cool!" Deen leaned in. "I can always use a marketing expert."

"I don't know if I wanna keep doing it," Evan admitted. "Most of my job was selling people crap they don't need by making them feel bad about themselves, or making a company like Monty's look important when it's damn well not."

There were a few moments of silence, and he cringed. *Way to kill the conversation, dude.*

"Wow. That's a good point," Nico finally said. "I'm sure we can help you figure out a way to use those skills for good, if you want. But I don't blame you for wanting to take a break."

"We all need that sometimes. Okay, I can feel Deen dying to tell us about this *small* wedding," Josh pointed out with a smirk. "And I need to know what dates you need what parts of the ranch."

"Is it being held there?" Evan asked.

Josh grinned. "Yep. A romantic winter wedding, he's finally decided. Final answer. Maybe. Unless he makes it a fall thing. Or next spring. Or renews his vows once every season…"

They were all laughing now, even Deen. "Shut up," Deen groaned. "It's not my fault your place looks pretty in all seasons."

Evan was happy to give up the spotlight for a while and listen to other people's plans, dreams, and problems. But they didn't exclude him, either—they all made an effort to include him and explain when they were talking about people he didn't know.

Eventually, Evan relaxed enough to stop waiting for the knife in his back, or the cutting comment he'd have to grit his teeth and smile through. This wasn't just fake-niceness to get ahead and use each other.

It was friendship. He had friends now—they made that perfectly clear. Yet he still felt differently about Josh than anyone else at the table.

He could lie to himself and say he wanted more friends, or he could admit the truth: that Josh didn't make him feel good in the platonic sense alone.

But the inevitable couldn't be ignored: it wasn't the right time. Why the hell did he have to meet this perfect guy and all his wonderful friends now? And perhaps the scarier question: what would have happened to him had he not met them right now?

It was either the best or worst timing of his life, but he couldn't figure out which.

CHAPTER

Twelve

JOSH

Where the hell had the weekend gone?

One moment, he'd been laughing at the bar with Evan and his buddies, and the next he'd been swamped in work. Now it was Sunday night, and one day closer to the next chapter in their life.

Lives. Not life. That implied… togetherness. And they weren't.

He'd never had this problem before. He'd been fine hiring friends of friends, or even people he'd known from back in school.

But Evan? He was different. Evan was under his skin, and Josh couldn't stop thinking about him, and the way he felt when he was tucked under Josh's arm.

His new friend was relaxing. He looked healthier and happier every day he was here. Hell, Evan smiled more in an hour than he had that whole first day. The country air and a bit of being spoiled was good for him, and Josh was glad to see it.

"What are we watching?" Evan came back with a bowl of

chips and two beers, grinning at Josh as he flopped onto the couch. Way closer than friends would, too—he sat right under Josh's arm, wriggling up against him.

Evan had suddenly become touchy-feely over the last couple of days, maybe as he grew more comfortable around Josh. It was literally fucking impossible for Josh to resist. He'd always been a physical guy himself, even with friends.

With those bright, curious eyes and that charming smile? He was screwed.

"Um," Josh answered to stall, sliding his arm around Evan's shoulders and accepting the bottle of beer. "I hadn't thought about it."

"Too busy daydreaming about work?" Evan gave him a disapproving look. "You know that's not good for you."

"Yes, sir," Josh teased, grinning when Evan blushed. God, he was so easy to embarrass. He shouldn't take advantage of it, he knew, but he couldn't resist that, either.

"I think I should be calling you sir."

"Oh, really?" Josh grinned.

The sexual tension between them was impossible to ignore, and it hadn't faded one bit. They'd traded a few more blowjobs and handjobs, but Josh had resisted sleeping with Evan. That seemed too intimate for something he was going to have to give up.

"In practice for tomorrow." Evan winked. "Or tonight."

Fuck. Just like that, Evan had Josh's cock standing to attention. One pretty little wink, one suggestive smirk of those plush lips, and he was putty in Evan's hands.

"What did you have in mind?" Josh's lips felt dry, so he licked them. Evan's gaze fell to watch Josh's tongue dart across his lips, and then flickered back up to his eyes.

"How about we make the most of our night?" Evan gestured toward Josh's bedroom.

Josh nodded before he let himself think about it. They'd messed around so much this week that one more time couldn't hurt.

It felt good, it was fun, and it gave him satisfaction to watch Evan opening up and becoming more playful.

They'd never done it in the bedroom, aside from that first time in Evan's cabin. The last week had been full of fumbling exploration in all the other rooms of the house, but by some unspoken agreement, they hadn't brought it to bed.

What was there to worry about? They both knew it wasn't serious.

"Sounds good," Josh said with a grin, ignoring the pesky voice of reason that said otherwise.

Evan caught his hand and pulled him to his feet, then led him to the bedroom. "I want to try something else tonight."

"I've created a monster," Josh teased. "What did you have in mind?"

Evan hummed, pretending to think. "That depends. Do you prefer to top or bottom? Both? Neither? We could try frot… or stick to what we're already doing…"

"Uh." The images that bombarded Josh all at once made his mind spin. Bending Evan in two and pounding him to the soundtrack of his whimpers and gasps? Feeling Evan crouched over and deep inside him, filling him to the limit? Taking turns at it? Evan's hot little mouth on his cock again, or Evan's cock lined up against his?

Josh had almost forgotten the question by now. "Everything."

"You're not picky, huh?" Evan laughed, throwing his arms around Josh's neck as soon as they reached the bedroom.

Josh steered Evan toward the bed with his body, nudging him.

"You're herding me like a sheepdog," Evan giggled, and he started trying to evade Josh. When Josh thrust his hips, he danced just out of reach, sidling around him in a maddening game of cat-and-mouse.

Josh growled. "You goddamn tease."

"You gonna lasso me if I misbehave?" Evan's eyes twinkled. God, he was the sweetest, most gorgeous thing Josh had seen. It almost took his breath away.

"I'd damn sure like to." When Evan sidled closer, Josh grabbed him by the waist and pulled him in roughly, catching his weight when he stumbled into him.

The squeaking noise Evan made was utterly adorable. "Hey!"

Josh grinned, pressing their hips together and grinding slowly. Evan's hard-on felt incredible, even through the layers of fabric—and he made sure Evan felt his, too.

"God, that's hot," Evan admitted a moment later, looping his arms around Josh's neck again. He finally leaned in, tilting his face in obvious surrender.

Despite the passion burning through him, Josh kissed Evan slowly. He sucked his lip gently, teasing with the tip of his tongue, and then his other lip, and then caught his tongue for the same treatment. Their lips slid together, rougher and faster this time, and Evan was soon gasping for breath.

By the time he pulled back, Evan's lips were swollen with kisses, and his eyes glazed in pleasure.

"That's a sexy look on you," Josh whispered. "I should make you wear it more often."

"Please." Evan's voice was breathless. "Please do."

Josh's heart hurt, and he wrapped his arms around Evan's

back, cradling him as he kissed his forehead. "Just say the word." He knew he ought to resist, or insist that he couldn't sleep with him, as his boss.

But, for once in his goddamn life, Josh wanted to be selfish. What could it hurt? Being friends with benefits was working so far. More sex was a good thing. And damn the consequences. He could deal with those later.

"Fuck me," Evan whispered. "Please. Make me feel good. I want you to use me hard, and hold me tight afterward."

With those words, Josh needed their clothes off—now.

He fumbled with Evan's shirt first, pulling it over his head in one clumsy motion. His own came off next, and then he unbuttoned Evan's pants.

Evan braced himself on Josh's shoulders as Josh sank to the floor along with Evan's clothing, until he knelt in front of him.

Every time he sucked Evan's cock, Evan looked like he wasn't quite sure he deserved it. Josh was as determined as ever to make him feel like he did.

Josh moaned his appreciation for the rock-hard, rosy pink shaft that tantalized his tastebuds. "Goddamn condoms."

"If you want to take the chance," Evan whispered. "I was only with Monty. And he said he wasn't with anyone else. I can't promise that he was telling the truth..." The way he said it, it was easy to tell that he feared Monty hadn't been. "But, um, I kept getting secretly tested. And everything's always been negative."

Josh nodded, his respect for Evan climbing a few notches. Not many guys would be practical enough to do that, let alone in secret when they suspected their boyfriend of being unfaithful. God, he was a hell of a smart guy.

He squeezed Evan's hip gently. "I wanna taste you," he whispered. "And I've only used condoms for everything, with everyone… for too long."

It wasn't like forgoing a condom was magically intimate. Hell, Josh found it *more* intimate when he could let go and just fuck to his heart's content. But this was different, and just like Evan, he craved something different from his routine.

Plus, cum tasted really fucking good, and he missed it.

"Yeah?" Evan smiled. "Sure."

"As long as you let me swallow."

Evan's moan turned into a gasp when Josh lapped from the base to the tip of his shaft. The velvety feeling of Evan's soft skin thinly covering his hard shaft, and Josh's lips sliding down over the head, was incredible.

He teased the head with his tongue, then bobbed his head slowly down and back up. Feeling Evan twitch under his hands and mouth and hearing the gasps of pleasure spilling from lips was a bonus.

After he was sure Evan was nice and turned on, Josh pulled his mouth away and stood up, grinning at the protesting sound Evan made. "What?" Josh teased.

Evan grabbed the sides of his head and hauled him in for a hard kiss. It was hard to focus on unbuttoning his own jeans when Evan kissed him like this—like the world was ending and they had this one chance to be together.

With Monday coming up, it kind of feels like it is.

Evan didn't say a word when he finally drew back and flopped on the bed. The inviting gaze he cast Josh said it all. Like a moth to the flame, Josh followed.

Evan folded his hands behind his head and stretched as Josh straddled him, wriggling to find a comfortable spot. The skin-on-skin contact felt incredible, especially with Evan's cock grinding against his.

"Oof," Josh moaned, shuddering with pleasure. The sparks that shot through him and danced across his skin made him grin. It felt surprisingly good to have Evan under him—and not just good. Right.

Evan reached down to wrap his long fingers around their shafts, squeezing them together.

Josh thrust a few times, their slick shafts gliding together. The squeeze of Evan's fingers around the top of his shaft and the pressure of Evan's cock against the bottom was just goddamn perfect.

He wasn't sure how much time passed as he ground against Evan. He felt young and clumsy all over again, like he'd never tried this before. And frankly, he hadn't often stuck with it.

In the last year or two of hookups, Josh had pretty much exclusively done handjobs if he didn't like the guy, blowjobs if he did, and anal because... well, because guys seemed to expect it.

Evan didn't seem to have expectations, though. He was always wide-eyed and fucking adorably eager for whatever the hell they ended up doing. But then again, Josh reminded himself, Evan had said himself that he was coming out of a drought. Anything had to beat that.

Any story Josh could tell himself to keep from wanting more, and getting hurt, was fine by him.

"Oh, God," Evan whispered, bringing Josh's attention crashing back to the present, and the overwhelming pleasure that was already burning through him.

"Good?" Josh murmured, slowing his pace.

"Yes! More," was all Evan seemed able to get out, urgently scrabbling at Josh's hip with his fingernails.

With that reaction, Josh wanted to grind against Evan until the night was over—or until they were rubbed raw, which sadly might happen first. Given enough lube, though...

He sped up again, letting Evan control how tightly to squeeze their throbbing cocks together as he braced his forearms on the bed and thrust.

Evan's panting cries of *Yes!* rang in his ears, spurring him on to kiss Evan's cheek and neck. He wanted to take his time and kiss Evan from head to toe, but orgasm was too close for both of them. If he stopped now, Evan was gonna have his balls.

"I'm so close," Evan moaned, and Josh pushed himself up on his hands so he could watch Evan's face. He looked gorgeous when he came—all hint of self-control and caution gone. Josh loved that Evan threw himself into sex with all the wild abandon he hadn't expected from a guy like him.

Josh wanted Evan. It was impossible to deny when they were so close, and when the way he touched him came damn close to making love.

But he couldn't have him. All he could have was his pleasure for a few nights—at best, a few months.

That had to be enough.

He pressed close to Evan, blanketing him to the bed and kissing him hard as he felt Evan spill first. Finally able to let go and give in to bliss, it only took him a minute more of thrusting into Evan's tight grip before he gasped and pressed his face into Evan's shoulder, groaning as his world narrowed to Evan.

Only Evan.

The fog was slow to lift, even when his breathing slowed and his heart rate returned to normal. He stayed pressed against Evan, and part of him couldn't bear to be separated. He needed something from Evan that he didn't quite understand.

He gradually became aware that Evan was touching him—rubbing his shoulders, back, and side. Murmuring to him. "That was so hot," Evan whispered, kissing his cheek. "Thank you. God, I needed that."

Affection. Intimacy. That was what he needed. He wanted to hold Evan close, and he was terrified that he'd just slip away.

But Evan was right there, smiling at Josh like he knew what he was thinking. Josh could trust him.

Josh rolled slowly off Evan and kissed his cheek, rubbing at his eyes. "Wow."

"Mmm," Evan agreed. When he rolled away, it was just to grab tissues to clean them up. "That was hot as hell."

"Do you..." Josh started, swallowing. His tongue felt clumsy now. "Do you wanna stay the night?"

Evan's eyes sparkled with amusement. "I hoped you'd let me. The hayloft would be itchy."

Josh grinned. "Shut up, you know what I mean." He gestured at his own bed. Then, the question occurred to him, and he asked, "How do you know that?"

"A lucky guess." Evan winked, wriggling under the covers.

Josh laughed. "I think you'll never stop surprising me." He spoke a little too carelessly, making assumptions he had no right to make, but Evan didn't correct him and he got high on it.

"And you me." Evan's gaze dropped to Josh's chest, and he rubbed it gently. Josh sensed he wanted to say something, so he held silent long enough for Evan to speak. "I... I really needed this."

"Me, too." Josh wrapped his arm around Evan as they shifted around, getting comfortable under the covers. The intimacy was unfamiliar after so many years spent leaving men's bedrooms ten minutes later, but it was important. Fulfilling.

"But I'm gonna be broken for a little while." Evan's voice was soft and vulnerable, making Josh pull him in even tighter. "I have a lot of feelings about Monty to work through. Not love—you don't have to worry about that. But he hurt me, and I'm... not okay yet."

"That's fine," Josh murmured. "We're all a little broken."

Evan looked at him quickly—too quickly, with too perceptive a gaze. He just said, "I know." After a few long moments, Evan fidgeted. "You don't have to do anything for me that you wouldn't otherwise."

Josh inspected Evan's arm, running his fingers slowly along it. "I've noticed you trying to manage me before. Smooth things out. Be less of a burden. Am I right?" He wasn't sure if he was going to earn a gasp or a slap.

Evan did neither. He just watched Josh closely for a few moments, his brow furrowed. "I guess so. The way I keep apologizing, and... yeah, feeling like a burden... I guess it *is* like I'm trying to control your reactions."

"You won't get a bad one from me, as long as you're not trying to be a dick," Josh promised. "And you don't have to hide your feelings about Monty. If I'm a rebound—" Evan started to speak, but Josh pressed a finger over his lips. "It *was* the agreement. And that's only fair to you. If I *am* a rebound, that doesn't mean this wasn't worth it. But I'd like to know, someday, if I'm not. Not yet. I can wait. But someday."

Evan looked too surprised to speak at first. Then, he slowly nodded. "I assumed…" he trailed off. A few moments later, he said, "That actually makes sense. Thank you." He stared off into space for a good minute, seemingly lost in thought except for the occasional, "Mm."

It wasn't the best place to end their conversation, but sleep was calling. Evan's eyes looked heavy, too. He kept closing them for a few seconds.

Josh leaned over to turn out the light, and Evan snuggled into his chest as soon as he lay down again.

It was probably cheating to ask Evan to sleep with him while he thought about whether they had a future, but Josh wasn't above playing a bit dirty. Ultimately, all that mattered was whether Evan kept liking Josh even when the image of Monty faded in his mind. And only time would tell, one way or the other.

Josh wasn't usually the most patient guy, but for this, his patience felt infinite. It would take time for Evan to know how he really felt, and they had that now. Evan had some stability for a few months, and a place to live, and fresh country air.

Already, he seemed much more himself—not that Josh had known him before, but he seemed more rounded, more whole as a person.

Josh could wait a long time for answers if he had the chance to keep getting to know this brighter, happier Evan in the meantime.

CHAPTER
Thirteen

EVAN

"Come on down to reception at nine. I'll get you to help with some grunt labor today." Josh's thoughts were clearly miles away. He shrugged on a thin plaid shirt over his undershirt, then buttoned up.

It was barely dawn, but Evan had already learned that Josh got up early. Even when he'd stayed up late, he seemed unable to stay in bed past sun-up.

"Of course." Evan quietly sighed as he watched Josh's gorgeous body disappear under layers of clothing. "Nine? I can start earlier. I've just got to clear up things with Monty."

"Nine's fine," Josh answered. "Not a lot will be going on before then. Animals gotta be taken care of, and then we'll have a couple free hands to help us check the fencing." He cast a sly grin at Evan. "You're light enough that we can share a horse."

Evan gulped. "Sounds good." He wasn't one for lying, but this was Josh speaking as his boss, so he was gonna speak like a new employee who was eager to impress. He just hoped he didn't make an ass of himself.

"We'll get you broken in," Josh promised and winked at him as he buttoned up his jeans.

Unable to resist flirting, Evan asked, "That a promise?"

"Hell, yeah." Josh raised a hand in a quick wave. "I'll put the coffee on."

"Thanks. I won't be in bed long," Evan said. Just thinking about signing that stupid contract had him wound up—he'd read it through, and yeah, nothing unexpected. Still, the principle pissed him off.

"See you in a bit."

It was strange being left alone in Josh's room. There were so many little reflections of him in the decor and the furnishings, but the main object of his interest left the house just a couple minutes later.

Evan sighed and pushed himself out of bed. It was way too easy to let himself slip into imagining that this was his new life now.

Living here, helping Josh manage the ranch in the daytime and spending nights of passion with him.

How fucking cheesy was that? His life wasn't some stupid movie where he got a happily-ever-after ending just because Josh had happened to be in the right place at the right time. More to the point, that kind of future for them would mean hard work on both of their parts.

Getting over Monty was one thing, but Josh clearly had his own reasons for keeping Evan at arms-length. It was clear that Josh wanted to be closer, and he didn't seem like the type to play mind games for no good reason.

A quick shower later, he headed to the living room to grab his laptop. Actually signing the document took thirty seconds—he was used to electronically signing PDFs from the very unpaid job he'd now been kicked out of.

He clicked the Send button as aggressively as he could, then huffed out a breath.

"Done."

It didn't feel done, though. Not for him. Maybe Monty could walk away this easily, but he couldn't.

He picked up his phone and called, before he could stop himself.

Monty sounded crisp and awake as always. "Monty speaking." He had caller ID. He knew damn well who was calling, but he was undoubtedly planning to give Evan the cold shoulder.

Evan didn't give him any satisfaction. "Morning. It's Evan. I sent over the contract and CC'd you. Did you receive it?"

"Yes. Excellent. My lawyer will be in touch." Even the way he said it was cold and aloof.

"About the cabin rental. I'd be happy to chip in, if you want." Evan felt it was only fair. He could ill-afford it, but he'd gone long enough not paying for things that he had *some* savings. And asking Monty to pay for that week was a bit too cheeky, even considering his asshole-ry about the whole situation.

"Hm? No, it's just a night. All I wanted from you was the contract."

And my work for years, and then to call me a freeloading scrounger. Evan barely managed to keep his response to himself. "Right. Fine. Bye." He hung up, hoping it sounded as pissed-off as Monty's voice made him feel.

Evan stalked to the kitchen for a cup of coffee. The only satisfying thing about that call was that he wasn't engaged to that prick anymore, thank fucking God.

As his anger cooled off, Evan furrowed his brows. *It's just a night* kept echoing in his mind. Something about that sounded wrong.

It didn't take long for him to put two and two together: Josh had said Monty had paid for a week, but then in the middle of the shoot when he'd passed by, he'd hinted that Monty had checked out early.

Which meant Josh had let him stay in the cabin rent-free and lied to him about it.

Evan blew out a sigh. He could see why Josh had done it; he wouldn't have accepted charity, after all. But lying to him was also not cool. If there was one thing that set his teeth on edge, that was it, and starting a new working relationship with Josh after finding this out was going to be a hell of a lot harder.

That was it. He was half an hour early, but he'd head down now and find Josh to straighten this out. The last thing he wanted was to leave something like this looming over their heads.

But how the hell was he gonna approach this without pissing off both himself and Josh, and ruining this fragile stability he'd found?

***

"You lied to me."

It sounded less confrontational with a joking grin. And he knew that by so carefully choosing what he said and how, he was doing just what Josh had told him—managing Josh's mood.

"Huh?" Josh looked up from the paperwork on his desk, then at the clock, then back to Evan.

Evan leaned in the doorway and shook his head. "The cabin. I put two and two together. It wasn't prepaid."

Josh's blush and guilty expression was confirmation enough, but he nodded once. "Yeah. I wouldn't have been able to find anyone else to rent the place anyway, on that short notice."

"Really? Or are you just making me feel better?" Evan probed, watching his expression carefully. He kept his voice down so the people working at the reception desk didn't overhear them.

Josh smiled. "Really," he said, and Evan believed him.

"Still. You should have told me."

The office phone rang, and Josh grimaced and glanced at it. Evan waved him towards it—he certainly wasn't presumptuous enough to interrupt whatever business stuff Josh was doing.

"Hello?" Then, Josh waved Evan inside and gestured for him to shut the door. "Hi, Adam. Yes, I was expecting you to be sick today. It's a sunny day, isn't it?" He paused, then said, "Yes, I am. And yes, I can do that. Tennessee is an at-will state, and I've given you many chances."

Even from across the office, Evan could hear the shouting from the other end of the line, and he winced.

Josh seemed unfazed. "You should be resting your voice. Come in tomorrow when you're feeling better and I'll cut your final check." Josh hung up and grimaced, running his hands through his hair.

Evan found he was holding his breath. "That was... the kid who never shows up?"

"Yep. I can't rely on him one bit. Season's getting slower, so I don't need the headache. I tried to give him chances. I hate firing people, but man, I had to. He practically did it himself." Josh's hands were still shaking, and Evan wasn't sure Josh was aware of that.

Evan approached him and squeezed his shoulder, then leaned on the edge of the desk. "I guess we can settle things later, about the cabin."

Josh seemed like he was only halfway paying attention. "If you wouldn't mind, yeah. Let's get out there and start checking fence posts." He bounced to his feet and led Evan out of the office at a brisk stride.

Evan had to trot to keep up with him. Suddenly, the relaxed and sheepish Josh he'd talked to a moment ago had given way to this steely man with a to-do list and nothing that could get in his way.

Josh glanced at him. "Hope you're up for a long day. We'll take a quick ride first to check out the perimeter. Hopefully there ain't much that needs fixing."

"I'm up for a long day," Evan retorted, sticking his chin out defiantly. He wasn't a loafing layabout loser like Monty wanted him to think, and he was damn well gonna prove it.

True to his word, Josh hoisted Evan up on the back of his saddle. "Quicker than leading one for you," he said simply. "Hold on tight."

Evan had no idea how much time passed as he desperately clung to Josh and kept his thighs tight around the saddle. When he heard a truck along the main road parallel to the field and Josh slowed the horse to a stop, Evan sent up prayers of thanks for the interruption. The awkwardly bouncing canter had grown old, with his worries about smashing his teeth out on Josh's shoulder blades.

"Hey, asshole. You fucking fired me!" The kid striding from the beat-up pickup truck toward the fence looked pissed, but at least he looked unarmed.

On the other hand, I'll take some tooth-to-skin contact now, Evan thought, remaining calm as Josh swung himself down from the saddle to approach the fence.

"Yeah, I did," Josh answered. He kept cool and calm, like he knew how to handle himself in a fight.

Evan gripped the saddle horn a little tighter as the horse shifted under him. He considered getting down, but that might put him at a disadvantage if things got ugly. As long as the horse didn't spook, he was fine, he told himself.

"Fuck you. You know I need this job!"

Moving almost without looking, Josh stroked the horse's cheek, then approached the fence. "You're not entitled to a job if you can't show up to work. That's the definition of work, kid. Trade time for work. Sooner you learn it, sooner your life will get better."

"Fuck you! And fuck you too. I bet you're the new guy, huh? To replace me?" Adam barked at Evan, flipping them both off. "Well, I'll tell them I ain't sucking the boss's cock. I don't give a shit anyway."

Evan fought to keep a lid on his anger. Meanwhile, Josh folded his arms, and Evan had to admit—even from horseback, he made an intimidating sight.

"Yeah, you don't care," Josh said. "That's why you drove all the way down here to yell at me across the fence for firing a guy who can't be fucking assed to show up to work half the time."

Evan bit back his grin. He had a point there.

Adam only got madder. He spat on the ground and flipped Josh off again, then stormed back to his truck, shouting things about how the ranch would fail and Josh could go die.

It was all Evan could do to keep his grip on the saddle and

not get off that horse and hunt the little twerp down. He breathed a sigh of relief when the pickup truck pulled away.

Josh stroked the horse's nose with one hand, and Evan's thigh lightly with the other. "Hey," he murmured, drawing Evan's gaze. "It's fine. Sorry about that. He's always had an attitude. Might've guessed he'd come run his mouth at me."

"Are you okay?" Evan murmured, glancing at Josh's hands. Not shaking, but he was still in that cool crisis-resolution mode. "That struck a nerve."

"What? I'm fine." Josh's response was so quick it had to be automatic.

Evan stayed put while Josh mounted like he was born to the goddamn saddle. When he'd stopped thinking about how hot that was, he wrapped his arm around Josh's waist. "Earlier, you were upset."

"Oh." Josh didn't say anything, but the way he shifted told Evan he knew what he was talking about.

"I'm just saying, you don't get to be that smart about why I'm the way I am without... well, personal experience." Evan didn't want to push his luck, but he had to say it.

Josh stiffened. "We'll talk later. Looks like a fence post needs mending over there."

"Oh?" Evan stifled his sigh as he added *why are you so afraid of conflict?* to his list of things to discuss after work.

The elephant in the room—the field?—was gonna make this a long day.

CHAPTER
Fourteen

JOSH

"Boss? You know who that guy is?"

Josh squinted out the window of the office and blew out a sigh. Nope, he didn't recognize the kid wandering around the cabins, kicking up dust. He looked young enough that he could have been someone's grown-up kid, but he could also be here on his own.

"Nah. He been here a while?"

"I dunno. Just saw him a few minutes ago, and he's wandering around like he's lost." Ryanna looked up at him. "Just letting you know."

Josh pushed his mental to-do list around. He was aching and sore from the morning replacing fence posts. First thing tomorrow, he and Evan were going to fix the fencing in that section, too.

All he wanted was a soak in the hot tub, preferably with Evan, but the place wouldn't run itself. He had all the tasks of a small ranch to oversee, plus those of a hotel. How the hell had he thought this would be *less* work than running a real ranch?

But then, he never could have stepped into his dad's shoes, and he hadn't wanted to. Hence taking off for the big city as soon as he could—for all of a couple years, until his dad had died.

Way too soon, by all accounts. He should have felt worse about it, but he'd never known how to describe the mix of feelings.

Anger at him, yeah, but betrayal, too. He was supposed to stay alive long enough for Josh to get the chance to reconcile with him. But that was another selfish thought, and as his dad had always told him, he was full of them.

Milk the cows before breakfast. Muck the stalls before supper.

No food or fun without chores. Even on sick days. Even on school days. Even on holidays.

These days, he was halfway inclined to agree with his dad, but going to school or bed—sometimes both—on an empty belly sucked. The alternative was making up excuses for why he hadn't done his homework when he didn't have time in the day, and school had always been his path out of here.

Until he'd come right back after barely three years away. And landed… here, with a staff looking up to him, and one eye on the account balances, the other on the future.

He needed a distraction, and he needed it now.

There was no point in dwelling on the past. Hell, most of his buddies had no idea how badly he and his dad had once fought. He sure as hell hadn't invited them over, and telling them was snitching. The old man had never liked that.

"I'll go have a word," he said and headed for the door. Fresh air brought him back to the moment, and his attention back to the kid he was going to talk to.

As soon as he saw movement, the guy turned on his heel

and made toward a cabin, but at a carefully measured ambling pace. It looked like he was walking with a purpose, but he wouldn't get there before Josh passed him. He looked carefully relaxed, and he didn't look at Josh.

That body language told Josh all he needed to know. Josh angled toward him, keeping his hands out of his pockets and back straight to radiate authority without being intimidating.

"Good evening," Josh greeted. He was deliberately polite, but he tried not to act too stiff and formal, either.

The kid jolted like he hadn't heard Josh and turned around, offering Josh a casual smile. "Hey."

"You need a hand finding anything?"

"No, thanks. I'm good." There was a certain defeated note to his voice, like he expected trouble.

Josh eyed him, then nodded around at the cabins. "Which one's yours?"

"Why?"

The answer confirmed Josh's suspicion. "You got a car here?"

The guy was silent, his dark eyes defiant as he gazed at Josh.

"Let me guess." It wasn't the first time it had happened. "You hitched a ride here, and you're here for business."

Other sex workers—once or twice, survival sex workers —had seen the gay-friendly flag and advertising online and made their way here, expecting a gay resort and easy money.

"We do it all on apps these days. Uber and Grindr are all I need." The guy folded his arms defensively. Josh fought back a smile. "What?" he added in a flat demand.

"Sorry. You just look like a hedgehog." His hair was spiky all over, and combined with the grumpy expression on his face, he might as well have been bristling all over. "It's a good look on you, but that hair could murder diamonds."

After a moment, he slowly smiled. "Are you calling the cops?"

"Hell, no." Josh shook his head. "I'm guessing you aren't paying your way through med school, though."

The guy snorted. "No. I'm not doing bad, but nobody wants to hire a nineteen-year-old without as much as a high school diploma."

"Piece of advice for you: lie." Josh sank onto the closest porch swing and patted the swing next to him, keeping some distance between them. He knew this cabin was empty, so they were unlikely to be interrupted.

Finally, the guy joined him. "Why? I don't like lying."

"I can tell." Josh grinned. It was pretty ballsy to as much as admit to the property owner that he was soliciting in the world's oldest profession. "But nobody really cares what high school you went to. Nobody ever checks it. They just wanna know that you can follow instructions."

"Oh."

After a moment of silence, Josh held out his hand. "Josh."

"Kev. I'm pretty bad at following instructions." Kev took Josh's hand and shook firmly.

"Are you? 'Cause, you know, you run your own business. That makes you a strong contender for getting shit done, even if you do things your own way. And I'm looking for another ranch hand. I'm not judging you, but if you're gonna do sex work, you should do it from a position of strength. Not because you need to make ends meet."

Kev eyed him as if deciding whether to trust him. Apparently he was satisfied with whatever Josh had already told him, because he nodded once. "Might be interested. Why do you wanna help?"

"I ask myself that some days," Josh muttered, his mind immediately back on Adam. But here he was, giving another young guy a chance to disappoint him. "Had to fire a guy who couldn't be bothered to show up for work. You've already beaten him in that department."

Kev laughed and relaxed a little.

"Where you from?"

"Knoxville. Or a bit outside it, anyway." Kev was vague, and Josh couldn't blame him. When he'd escaped to college for his couple years away, he hadn't wanted to talk about where he came from.

Josh nodded. "Got a place to stay?"

"A friend's couch, for a couple more nights." Kev shrugged. "I'll figure it out."

"Is it the classic *need a credit record and a guarantor and a first-born to get an apartment* thing? That's a shitty one. I rented with some buddies," Josh told him.

"That, and needing a job to get a place, but needing a place to get a job."

Josh had never been in that particular scenario, but he could imagine it easily enough. Dad hadn't been supportive of him moving out, but he hadn't thrown him out, either.

The idea had occurred to Josh before, but he turned it over in his head a few times. "Well... peak season has passed for us. We're gonna have vacancies until spring. I can put aside a cabin for you—but you might have to share if any other ranch hands need a place."

Kev looked suspicious. "That's awful nice."

"But you have to promise—no solicitation on my premises," Josh added, nudging Kev's foot with his own. "I don't wanna get in trouble any more than you do. I don't care what you do for free, if you're over eighteen—you are, right?"

"Got the driver's license to prove it. And I was practically born on a tractor."

"That makes you even handier." Josh needed someone who could drive farm equipment. "I need a little faith in people right now. Don't let me down, man."

Kev's expression shifted to concern, and he looked like he wanted to ask if Josh was okay. He held his tongue, though, and just nodded.

Good thing, too. Josh wasn't sure how he would have answered. "As for why I'm doing this…" he trailed off, looking around the place. He could still see the place without the cabins, and with more fencing and animals and machinery. It hadn't been a kid-friendly place to grow up. "Absolution or something, I guess. That's my five-dollar word of the day."

Kev nodded slowly. "Well, I appreciate it."

Josh rose to his feet. "Wanna come to dinner with me and my bo—" he cut himself off. *Oh, shit. I nearly called him my boyfriend.* "And my, uh, friend? We can talk about the job, salary, living arrangements, all that stuff."

"Your uh-friend?" Kev teased. He had a wicked streak in him, and Josh liked that. Employees who kept their eyes on the ground and were too *yes-sir* didn't spot problems or come up with solutions, or even really care about the place.

He wanted someone with a mind of their own. A lot like the edges and playful attitude Evan was starting to show. Evan had buckled down and worked hard today, and Josh somehow wasn't surprised.

Maybe hiring from the heart wasn't a bad idea after all.

"Yeah." Josh chuckled. "If you've got other plans, we can

meet up tomorrow morning at nine at the reception."

"Dinner sounds great," Kev said after a moment. He reached out to shake hands, and the smile that crossed his face was genuine. "Thank you, Josh. I totally didn't expect this, but… I hope it works out."

"Me, too." Josh shook hands again and clapped Kev's shoulder. "Gimme ten minutes and come on up to my place —it's the one up there."

"I'll do that."

As far as Josh was concerned, he'd come out better from their deal. He'd pay Kev a little less than the other staff but cover the costs of his housing and bills. He wouldn't have to check up on an unoccupied cabin so often. And after the autumn, with savings and a steady job, Kev would find it a lot easier to get a place of his own. Win-win.

Plus, it saved him having to train someone who'd never been around a ranch. This would free up Evan to put his talents to better use and promote the ranch. That would get some more business and help him cover both the new guys' salaries. That made… what, a win-win-win-win?

Or he could face the fact that he could jump through a million hoops to try to justify it, but that decision had been made from the heart. And because of it, the spark that had been missing from his daily routine was back again.

He offered getaways from reality for people, but he never felt like he was making a difference in someone's future. Not until Evan, and now Kev.

For the first time in months, Josh whistled as he walked up the path to his house. And, for the first time ever, he anticipated not just dinner in the oven, but a *hello* kiss from Evan at the door.

His steps sped up as he headed home.

CHAPTER
Fifteen
EVAN

Josh bounded through the door. "Honey, I'm home!"

The teasing grin made Evan roll his eyes. "Someone's in a good mood," he said, gesturing toward the kitchen. "Supper's ready."

And finally, he'd have a chance to talk to Josh about honesty and his own pride. It had been a long damn day, with all those thoughts rattling around his head.

Nobody wanted to feel like a charity case, after all. And hearing that Josh had covered the cost of a cabin rental for him to—what, stop moping around? It wasn't like he'd been contributing anything valuable. Unless it was a cheap way of getting a hookup, which he didn't believe of Josh, but…

After a few hours, with Monty's cruel parting words in his head, his doubts crept in.

"Ah. About that. Is there enough for three?"

Evan blinked in surprise. "Who are we expecting?"

Josh flopped on the couch next to him and put his arm around Evan's shoulders. "Good news." He leaned in for a kiss.

It was impossible to be annoyed at that puppy-like enthusiasm. Evan hadn't seen Josh in this mood before. He'd always been the solid, unexcitable rock through Evan's last week or so of life upheaval.

Evan pecked Josh's lips. "What?"

"His name's Kev." Josh took Evan's hand and placed it on his stomach. "I just found out."

Evan swatted Josh's shoulder. "I'm sure I'd remember that, you know. Hey, did you ever, like, get jealous of trans guys? I did when I realized they can skip surrogacy *and* have a baby with both guys' DNA." Evan had often thought about having kids with Monty, but all the details to straighten out had put him off.

"Oh, shit, yeah." Josh hummed. "If I wanted kids some-day… I mean, not that I don't… Wait. Are we having that conversation now?"

"No, that's a conversation for later." Evan laughed. Something had Josh in a very good mood, and he wanted to know what that was.

"My DNA's probably too lazy to get anyone pregnant anyway," Josh said with a snort.

Evan elbowed him. "No, it's not. Shut up. What's this about Kev? Get to the point."

Josh laughed. "Okay, God. Hold on." He bounced to his feet. "Supper for three?"

"Yeah, that's fine."

"Great! Kev's a runaway, I think. Looks about twenty, maybe gay. He was trying to solicit business at the cabins. I'm checking ID before I hire him, but… I'm hiring him. Conditional on him *not* trying to sell himself on Grindr on my property, where we'd all get in trouble. I invited him for supper, by the way."

Evan blinked a few times as Josh trotted to the kitchen, humming under his breath. That was a lot of information to take in at once, and it jarred. He was already feeling a bit like a pity case, but...

Now he just felt strange.

Was Josh moving on to his next sob story? Was he the kind of guy who just rescued people and then moved on when he couldn't save them from anything anymore?

After a minute of rattling dishes, Josh poked his head in the living room again. "The stew looks great. You okay?"

"Just... taking that in." Evan didn't want to be the pin pricking the bubble of Josh's happiness, but he had a hell of a lot of feelings hitting him at once. He finally managed a smile. "So you gave a guy who needed a job... a chance. Again. Like me."

Josh sucked in a breath, then headed toward him. "Yeah. Are you okay with that?"

"Oh, you have to keep hiring people, I know." Evan had heard Josh complain about his staff enough to figure that out. It seemed like he had a core staff who stuck around, but the others were flaky. "I don't wanna stop you doing that. That'd be dumb," he said and laughed.

Even to his ears, it sounded a little off.

Josh came to sit next to him again, taking his hand. "But?"

This was the side of Josh who would deeply listen to him. He recognized it easily, and he wished he hadn't needed that listening ear so often in the last week.

Evan took a deep breath and let it out. "I just... feel like a charity case. A pity fuck... or hire... or something. I know, you'll say that you need the help around here. But..."

"I do," Josh nodded, his eyes intent on Evan. "But?"

"But you lied to me about the cabin being paid for."

Josh's eyes lit up in recognition. "Ohhh. Right. I was gonna talk about that. And then…" he waved a hand toward the ranch. "Today passed."

"And you found another stray." Evan didn't mean it to sound so bitter, and he wasn't even sure what—or who—he was angry at.

Josh frowned. "Whoa. You're not just a—a stray. That's underselling yourself, dude."

"I know." When Evan tried to be reasonable, he did understand that much. He was here to work and help, not just take.

Oh. That was it.

"It's back to Monty," Evan mumbled, finally letting out his breath and resting his head on Josh's shoulder. "When he said I'm… you know, mooching off him. And then I felt like I'm mooching off you…"

Josh squeezed him around the shoulders. "You know you're not. And I'm not taking in strays just to feel good about myself. You know how hard it is to find someone who'll work worth a damn these days? Now I get why my dad used to…"

He trailed off, and his voice caught. Only for half a second before he went on, but Evan knew him well enough now to detect a hint of fake cheer in his voice.

"He used to complain about all the help around here."

"Including you?"

Josh caught his breath, his head whipping around as he looked at Evan.

There was a knock on the door, and they lost the moment. *Goddamn it,* Evan fumed. *I'll never get him to talk now.*

"That'll be Kev." Josh stood up again, and Evan did, too.

He noticed how quickly Josh headed for the door, so he went for the kitchen to ladle the stew into three bowls.

He was just coming here for a simpler life—to get away and figure things out. So how had things started to become tricky?

I guess that's life.

"Hi," he greeted Kev when he brought the bowls to the dining room table, which he'd already set earlier. Josh had added a third setting.

It was just one day of sharing dinner with someone, he reminded himself. Not the end of the world. They'd have a chance to talk later. And now, maybe—just maybe—he could get Josh to spill the beans.

Kev was pretty, young, thin, blond. All the things Evan had learned to see as competition for Monty's time and attention. But Josh wasn't like that, he reminded himself. Or rather, he hoped.

"Hi. I'm Kev."

He had a delicate grip when they shook hands, and he moved like he wasn't quite sure of himself. Had Evan moved like that at first? When he felt like the world was shifting around him? Kev glanced between the two of them, no doubt drawing his own conclusions.

I should be so lucky. Hell, if Josh did want to date Kev, what business was it of his? Evan had made it clear he was rebounding and not committing to anything with Josh. If Josh wanted commitment, he should get some from wherever he could. It just made sense.

The thought made Evan's stomach tight, but he tried to push through it.

"Evan. I'm staying here. I'm the second-newest employee, it sounds like." Evan offered a smile. He wasn't gonna be a dick to him. No point in making everyone's day harder.

"I hope so." Kev glanced at Josh, then took a seat at the table.

In the chair Evan usually sat in.

Evan gritted his teeth for a moment before he saw the humor of the situation. Here he was being jealous of a kid who was clearly in desperate need of a place to live and a job—more so than he even had been.

He could look at this another way: he could focus on Josh's big heart, for letting him in and giving him a chance, and doing the same for Kev.

God knew where he'd be otherwise. Probably Vermont at some crappy gas station job, figuring out if he still had what it took to work at an ad agency and sell payday loans and sham diet pills.

"Smells great. Thanks," Kev told them both, looking between them.

Josh grinned. "That's all Evan. I'll keep him around for a while," he joked, his voice light. But under that, there was something deeper. Josh wasn't the kind of guy to say that if he didn't mean it.

Evan relaxed and smiled as he brought the bread to the table and took a seat. "It's my pleasure. I used to do it a lot for, uh, my ex and me." He glanced at Kev. No sense in bringing up his biggest problem right away. "It's been nice to get back to it."

"Yeah. I don't get the chance to cook a lot," Kev said. "Sometimes for my friends when I'm staying with them."

"The cabins have kitchenettes and mini-fridges. It's not a lot, but it should help get back to some normalcy." Josh dug into his stew without further ado, his appetite fueled by a day's hard work.

Evan ate a little slower. His body ached after a morning on horseback and an afternoon helping Josh work the saw to cut new fence posts. It was a satisfying ache, though—one that told him he was making a real difference. He could see his work, piled up behind the wood shop.

They chit-chatted about the ranch setup and layout as they ate, and Kev asked good questions—smart ones, like how many horses they had, and how the guests' presence affected the ranch operations.

"So," Josh finally said. "I'll give you a straight-up deal. Forty hours a week of whatever odd jobs I can find for you. I might get you trained in tourism or hospitality work, or carpentry, or… whatever you have an interest in and I need done. I'll reduce your pay slightly compared to my usual starting salary, to account for allowing you a cabin."

Kev nodded. "All fair. But, uh… aren't you gonna ask?"

Josh blinked at Kev. "Ask?"

"Why I need a job and a place to live. Usually people wanna know. Do I have a record, or a baby mama…"

Josh half-smiled and shrugged. "Doesn't make a difference. Lots of good people end up in hard situations for reasons that are or aren't their fault. Hell, making a mistake shouldn't condemn anyone to fall through the cracks. Don't get me wrong… I'll let you go faster than you can say *fuck you* if you screw me over. I expect you to work hard, like any of my guys. But if you wanna work and you pass the ID checks, why not?"

Evan's respect grew a few notches. He'd gotten that sense from Josh already about himself, but seeing him apply it to someone else made it sink in. It wasn't just him—and it wasn't about getting anything from him in return.

Josh just wanted to help people, and Evan loved him a little for it.

"Thank you." Kev's gratitude was slow, almost cautious. He looked like he didn't quite believe Josh, but he was trying to do so.

I know the feeling, Evan reflected.

"You're welcome. So, come by the office tomorrow and I'll go over the paperwork and we'll figure out some kind of lease or agreement for the cabin. I have to talk to my insurance people and whatever," Josh waved a hand. "Are you fine for tonight?"

"Oh, yeah. Yeah, I've got a good couch." Kev scrambled to his feet. He was smiling now, looking more at ease—even eager. Again, a mirror of how Evan felt. It was strange to see on someone else, so soon afterward. "See you tomorrow. Nine?"

"Nine works. Thanks."

"Thanks for supper, Josh, Evan." Kev waved and strode out of the house like a man on a mission.

Evan chuckled quietly as he watched him go. "Not a lot of people would have turned the situation around like that, you know. Getting him out of that life."

When Josh closed the door, Evan realized they were standing side-by-side to see him off through the door, like an old married couple.

He stepped away and rubbed his cheeks, trying not to blush at the thought.

Josh shook his head. "It's just being compassionate. Everyone should. I'm not pitying him, or judging him. Hell, if he wants to go right back to sex work, that's his choice. But he should *have* a choice in the matter."

"Yeah." Evan sidled closer to Josh again and rested the side of his head on Josh's shoulder, slipping his arms around his waist. "Still. Thanks, on his behalf. And mine."

"I don't do it for thanks." Josh sounded vaguely uncomfortable as he rubbed Evan's back.

Evan smiled and tightened his hold. "I know." *That's why I love you for it, you doofus.* "I have my guesses about why, like I said."

Josh hesitated, and then took Evan's hand and led him to the couch. Was this it? Were they about to have a moment? Evan tried not to get overexcited, just cast Josh a curious look. It was his turn to listen.

"Dad didn't exactly kick me out," Josh chose to lead with, and a rush of breath left Evan's lungs.

"Well," Evan managed. "I'm glad for that." He curled into Josh's side, his arm around his waist now.

"Me too. But he did make it clear I should do something with my shiftless, lazy ass, so I took it off to college."

"You're neither of those things," Evan insisted, eyeing him.

Josh half-smiled. "Yeah, yeah. We never see in ourselves what other people do, huh? I see what he means, though. Where I could be better—do more. So maybe I'm overcompensating by using this place to give people opportunities, rather than stealing people's dreams." Josh stopped, looking surprised for a moment at what he'd said.

Evan wanted to squeeze the daylights out of him, but he refrained and just gently rubbed his chest. "Oh?"

"I—I'm happy here." Josh sounded less certain of that. "Especially when I have days like today. Giving people a job.

Giving other people a break from their life. Giving people a taste of a whole different life. Maybe some of them will take it back with them—spend less time on their crackphones and more in nature. Maybe not, but at least I'll have tried."

Evan hummed. "But this wasn't your dream?"

"Ouch." Josh laughed softly, his arm snaking around Evan's shoulders. "Yeah, it wasn't. At least, not as a fully-fledged ranch, like it used to be. Dad died, I came home, scaled the biz down, added the cabins, made it a dude ranch. Thought it'd be less..."

Less what, he didn't seem to quite know. He opened and closed his mouth a few times, then huffed in frustration.

"Less triggering of those memories?" Evan tried. It seemed to be the right answer, because Josh stared at him.

"Yeah. I guess. I mean, it wasn't an *un*happy childhood."

The fact that he was even clarifying that set Evan's nerves on edge, but he wasn't about to question Josh on it. "But there was conflict. That's enough to give any kid anxiety," he said, chuckling. "My parents were pretty happy, but I know people whose parents got divorced, or whatever."

Josh nodded. "Mom died when I was pretty young. Dad was a single parent. He ran the whole place, and tried to raise me. He had a lot on his plate."

"That's admirable," Evan managed, even if he had his doubts. Clearly, Josh admired the man as much as he... feared him? Was frustrated by him? Evan couldn't tell, and he suspected even Josh didn't know for sure.

"Yeah. Yeah, it is. I get now how much work it must have been." Josh looked at him. "If he got a little shouty sometimes, that ain't automatically abuse, you know?"

"There's a lot of gray areas," Evan said quietly, resisting the emotion that swelled in his chest. He saw the childlike need for validation in Josh's eyes when he looked at him like this, as if seeking confirmation that he'd turned out okay. "The world isn't black and white. People sure as hell aren't."

"Yeah." Josh let out a breath, and for the first time, he laid his head on Evan's shoulder.

Evan turned his face to kiss the top of Josh's head, then rested his cheek against Josh's hair, giving him a few moments of quiet to think about all the things he'd just admitted.

"I get the feeling I don't like conflict and shouting. Maybe because of all that," Josh murmured. "It gets me on-edge. Like I just can't settle down."

Evan hummed. "That makes sense."

"So I try not to shout at people. Even when guests get worked up and shout at me." Josh scoffed under his breath. "It's just a vacation. The number of people who can't stand that the right flowers aren't in bloom, or they don't have a pizza pan in their kitchenette…"

"Oh, God." Evan laughed. "I bet."

"Anyway, it's not really important."

"No," Evan interrupted immediately. Josh had done that enough for him—he owed him as much in return. "*You* are important. Thinking about this stuff is hard, and talking about it… I'm glad you could trust me enough to do that."

"I don't tell a lot of people." Josh's voice was thick. "Even back then."

"Your, uh, significant brothers?"

Josh slowly shook his head. "I don't know why. The longer I've carried it around with me, the more of a big, dark secret it seemed. Even though I don't feel like it's that bad. But then, other people's parents let them—you know, do stuff my dad never would have tolerated. They don't seem afraid of the same stupid shit I am."

Evan cradled him against his shoulder, his chest aching for Josh—and the younger Josh he could hear in his voice. "I'm sorry, baby. You turned out to be a hell of a guy, though. You don't have to hold onto whatever shit other people have told you about yourself."

"Even my dad?"

"Even your dad," Evan murmured. "Even my ex-fiancé."

"Touché." Josh slowly sat up, and then wrapped his arms around Evan in a fierce hug. "Thanks. For… listening. I've never said any of that before. Always felt like whining."

"It's not." Evan hugged him back just as tightly, trying to keep his feelings in check. Crying on Josh's shoulder wouldn't encourage him to talk about it again. "You've heard me talking out all this shit lately. Otherwise it won't get out of your head, and then it just builds up. Like it has for you. Like it did for me, for years. And you've listened to me."

"Feels different, listening to someone else's problems. I feel luckier when I do," Josh admitted, laughing softly. "Like, I own my own business. That alone means I'm pretty damn lucky. If I can share that luck…"

"That makes you a pretty good catch," Evan teased.

"I know people who'd disagree." Josh grinned. "So!" He cleared his throat, clearly trying to draw a line under that conversation. He sounded hoarse and tired, which was about the stage Evan was at. "You got any energy left?"

"I could sleep standing up," Evan admitted, laughing. "You beat me out today."

"Bed?"

"Bed."

By unspoken agreement, they rose together and headed

for Josh's room together. No way in hell Evan was gonna let Josh be alone.

And when they lay together under the covers, Evan scooted up against Josh's back, pulling him in tightly against his front, kissing the back of his neck.

"I care about you," he murmured. It was the closest he could come to what he was starting to suspect—which was way too much, too soon.

Josh chuckled quietly, his hand covering Evan's. "Yeah. You, too." He twisted in Evan's hold to kiss him once, and then settled down to fall asleep.

Evan stayed awake for long minutes afterward, listening to the clock ticking, Josh's breathing evening out, the frogs in the pond outside, and his own thoughts racing around his head.

Maybe this wasn't a charity case. Maybe he could do as much for Josh as Josh did for him. And maybe—just maybe—the timing wasn't all wrong.

Maybe the timing was perfect.

Josh was convinced that coffee was the best drug ever invented. To hell with all the illegal shit—all he needed was a hit of caffeine every morning. And maybe one mid-afternoon, to top up the levels in his bloodstream.

With Evan around, he had more energy naturally than he had in years, though. Maybe it was all the sex. That couldn't hurt. Hadn't people always thought sexual energy was some magical force behind getting stuff done?

Over his second cup of coffee, sitting side-by-side with Evan at the breakfast counter, Josh finally had the energy and the brain power for the conversation that they'd come so close to yesterday.

"So, you wanted to talk about the cabin... rental... thing. Is now a good time?"

Frankly, if they went another day of avoiding the talk, he was going to explode from anxiety.

Evan was halfway through cramming a slice of toast in his mouth—not his most graceful look. He gave Josh a startled glance, then rolled his eyes and pointed at his mouth.

"Not this second," Josh grinned. "I have a few minutes before I gotta get to work. The boys take care of the horses. Reception always runs smoothly. I'm really... what's the word... superfluous?"

In truth, he didn't need to supervise people as closely as he did. At least, not the ones who he trusted to do the work —and right now, he was hoping that was all his staff.

"Mmm." Evan swigged his coffee, and then nodded. "Yeah. So. It kind of bothered me, until I saw how you handled Kev. I don't feel as much like a charity case anymore."

Josh relaxed a little. However ready he was for the conversation, knowing there wasn't conflict made it a lot easier. "Good. I should apologize, then."

He was getting awfully familiar with Evan's surprised face. "You should?"

"Yeah. I should've done this last night, really. I don't like going to bed without setting things right." Josh cradled his cup of coffee near his chest as he watched Evan. "I did lie to you that the cabin was paid for. Monty paid for the first night upfront but I gave him the refund on the rest. I didn't want his lawyers getting in touch," he admitted, crookedly smiling at Evan.

"Ah." Evan glowered at his remaining piece of toast. "Fucking lawyers."

"Now I kinda wish I'd made him fight for it more, but... hindsight is twenty-twenty," Josh said and sighed. "Anyway, it really wasn't any trouble for me, letting you stay there. Or the room tab. I've eaten more costs when a guest decides to be a dick and trashes the place."

Evan nodded. "But I still feel like... like I should pay you back." He sounded tentative.

"I'm not billing you," Josh grinned. "Nice try."

"Are you paying me more than Kev?"

Josh blinked and nodded. "For the extra skill set, yes." A good marketing guy cost way more than he was paying Evan, but then, he didn't know how good Evan was yet.

"Knock off the same amount from my pay as you knocked off Kev's for having room and board." Evan's chin stuck out when he was being stubborn, and it was distractingly adorable. "Then we'll call it even. Since I *am* getting the same—better, even."

"Fair enough." Josh nodded. "If it makes you feel better, then yeah. That's more than reasonable."

"But if you lie to me again, even for my own good, I'm gonna be pissed." Evan smiled at him. "I know you sensed I wouldn't take the offer if you'd made it, and I can't be too angry. I did benefit. But I don't like being lied to any more than feeling dependent. It's paternalistic."

Josh winced. "Yeah," he nodded. He wasn't completely sure what that word meant, but he guessed it was something about feeling like he was babying Evan. And he'd cop to that. "Yeah, I get it. You're right."

Evan slid his arms around Josh. "Good. Hug it out, bro."

"If you insist." Josh laughed and put down his coffee mug to return the hug. He was still a little disoriented, on edge and waiting for some bigger consequence. For Evan to swear at him and call him a shithead, or… he didn't even know what. Take away his toys? Send him to bed without supper?

This is different, he reminded himself. *He's nothing like my dad. Thank God. That would be weird.*

"I'm still gonna feel too dependent on you," Evan admitted, "but paying rent will help."

Josh pulled back and nudged Evan's coffee cup toward

him. "You know, a farm is like an ecosystem. Hay grows, we cut it down, we feed the horses, the horses carry us around, the manure goes back on the fields…"

Evan chuckled. "Are you giving me the interdependence lecture?"

"Maybe." Josh thought about the word for a few seconds and then nodded firmly. "We all rely on each other. Hell, you're living here, but you've been cooking me supper."

"That's just a nice guest thing to do." Evan smirked. "Plus, I get the feeling you'd forget to eat."

"Uh…" Josh flushed with heat and rubbed the back of his neck.

Evan grinned. "Gotcha. See, we mere mortals who aren't juggling a hundred things can take care of the little stuff, like getting you to eat."

"And getting me to sleep," Josh added with a wink.

Evan's hand wandered up his thigh. "Especially that."

God, they worked together so well. It was as natural as breathing, being around him. Why the hell couldn't it just stay like this?

But Josh was pretty sure that Evan would get bored of life here. Sure, this was exciting for the first few days. But by the end of a couple weeks, any new ranch hand from the city got tired of the mud and smell of horses and the guests constantly getting underfoot and asking stupid questions. "Are the horses local?" was his favorite one.

Sure, there were a lot of things to love about the farm— but maybe it wasn't about that. Maybe his insecurity had more to do with him.

How long before Evan got bored of him being out in the fields from dawn to dusk, sunburned in the summer and nursing cold fingers in the winter? How long before he decided he could get back to the city and all its excitement and fashion sense?

"Mmm. Save that thought for later," Josh said with a wink. "I gotta get out there and see how things are going. I know a couple people wanted early check-outs." He liked to be around to wish them well. He tended to get more repeat business when he took the time to build personal rapport with guests.

"Are we still on for fence post repairs?"

Josh considered it for a moment. "Well... how about we chat about that in my office before Kev comes by?" He had some numbers he wanted Evan to see before he made this request. He knew it was a big one, and he wasn't gonna ask without good reason.

Evan had said a couple times that he didn't want to get back into marketing. But it was, without a doubt, the most valuable thing he could do for the whole business.

Was this a different kind of project than he was used to? Josh could only hope so.

Evan shot him a puzzled look but nodded. "Sure. Be down soon."

If he says no, it's not like I can't find a place for him somewhere else. Josh's thoughts carried him out the door and down to the office after he checked in with Ryanna. At least this was motivation to go over the accounts—especially before he made yet another offer of employment.

More work done around here meant more appeal for guests, but only to a point. He was gonna have to get Kev on the till in the shop now that Adam was gone, but he didn't know if he could trust him with money yet... Evan could definitely be trusted, but was a lot more valuable behind the scenes. What about pulling Jordan from the barn for the morning, at least? He could hop on the till later and close out.

God, his life felt like a balancing act, but having a couple new guys around was invigorating.

One guy in particular put a smile on his face as he paged through the boring-ass accounts with his calculator and another cup of coffee, waiting for him to show up.

Around half an hour passed before there was a light knock on the door and Evan poked his head inside. "Hey, boss," he greeted with a lopsided grin.

Josh liked that he tried to respect the space between them when they were on the clock. Josh sucked at doing that. Keeping his hands off Evan was hard whenever they were in the same space. Even in a non-sexual way, Josh just wanted to hold him, or kiss him when he said something particularly smart, or horse around as he teased him. He was fun to tease. In every possible way.

Focus, goddamn it, Josh thought. He couldn't be imagining screwing Evan when he had a business to run, and a tough conversation to have. "Hey! Sit down, close the door."

"Yessir." Evan took a seat and leaned forward, looking nervous.

"I was thinking about what jobs to assign you and Kev. Both of you are pretty new and need training, but you've got different skills. Kev grew up around farm equipment, and…"

"I didn't," Evan finished with a rueful smile. "Yeah. Sorry."

"Oh, no need to apologize." Josh waved it off. "I hire kids all the time who don't know what they're doing. But you've also got a lot of skills he doesn't."

"The skillset you mentioned earlier. Marketing." Evan nodded slowly. "What about it?"

"Well… how did you and, uh, you and Monty find out

about this place?" It felt weird to bring up his ex-fiancé in casual conversation.

"Google, I think. Or TripAdvisor. I was just looking for a good place to get away. Somewhere exotic, but American. Maybe I searched Wild West… I definitely searched for gay-friendly places." Evan looked like he was thinking it through already. "You want more business?"

"I need more business," Josh corrected him. He didn't want to make it sound like a crisis, but… "I've been looking over the books, and every week this year, business is down over last year. It's not like I have to start letting people go, but… profits are slimmer, and those cabins ain't all paid off yet."

Evan sat up straight, a gleam in his eye. "You want me to come up with a marketing plan?"

"Well, you said you were out of the business." Josh hesitated. "I didn't want to ask you to do something you're not comfortable with. But if you can…"

"It's no problem." Evan spoke confidently, his back straightening. This was a side of him he hadn't quite seen before. "I just hated marketing when it was all strategic meetings with CEOs, and empty business speak, and selling people crap they don't need. But I'm sold on the reinvigorating powers of a trip like this."

Relief rushed through Josh, and he offered a smile. "I also didn't want you to feel that, um…"

Evan waited, his brow raised.

"That…" Josh fidgeted. "I was using you?"

Evan paused, then chuckled. The reaction was unexpected, so Josh stared. Evan clarified, "*You* were using *me*?"

"Ah." Josh laughed and shook his head. "I guess we both have to get over that feeling."

"We've only known each other a week and a half," Evan said, leaning across the desk and taking his hand. "But I know the kind of man you are. You've shown me that in the little moments as well as the big ones."

Josh blushed. The compliments from him were hard to handle. "What you see is what you get. My best friend—Ty—and I are both like that. It can put people off."

"You ain't putting me off so easily, mister," Evan drawled, imitating his accent for just a moment. It made Josh crack up.

"Okay. So you're fine with the plan?"

"Doesn't seem fair to poor Kev, but yeah," Evan said and chuckled. "If he wants some physical labor, I think he's just as skinny as me."

"Oh, this isn't it for your manual labor," Josh promised and grinned. "I'll get you both beefed up by the end of the winter."

Evan squeezed one of his biceps and sighed. "Please do."

There was another knock on the door and Kev poked his head in. He was dressed in much less fashionable clothes today—a plaid shirt and scuffed jeans. "Hey. Um, I'm a bit early, but I'm here."

"Perfect timing. I just figured out what your first day's gonna be about. Hope you're ready to work," Josh greeted with a grin.

Kev nodded once, hard. There was a glint of determination in his eyes, much like in Evan's. "Oh, yeah. I'm ready."

"Let's get this contract signed."

Evan stood up. "I'll head up to the house and grab my laptop. I need to start looking at the market before I can do anything. And I'll need some numbers from you."

"Help yourself," Josh said, gesturing around the office. "Whatever's not here, ask me on my lunch break."

"Awesome." Evan beamed at him and slipped out, and Kev took his place.

The energy was easy to feel: the kind of spark that came with a good plan. Maybe—just maybe—Josh had finally found people he could count on.

He hadn't felt like part of a team for a long damn time, but now… he had the beginnings of one. Everyone still on staff was someone he trusted to do their job.

This would be the winter he turned things around. He'd figure out how to make it all work—the business, the relationship with Evan, the apprenticeship with Kev—and maybe other young guys, if he could find any who were as willing to work hard and learn as Kev seemed to be.

And it had all started with one man throwing up on his shoes.

Who'd have thought?

CHAPTER
Seventeen

EVAN

Out-of-state tourism?

Evan chewed on the end of his pen, staring at his notepad. He added a few more words. *Travel bloggers, partnerships, LGBT directories.*

He wasn't convinced he had all the answers for Josh yet, but he had a few more puzzle pieces, at least. He'd had to grab Josh a few times that day to clarify numbers: how many rentals there had been over the last few years, in which weeks, and what the available add-ons were.

It took all he had not to calculate the final bill for his stay and activities, as footed by Josh. They were past that, he reminded himself.

Just as he started to Google LGBT directories where they could list the ranch, his phone went off. Maybe it was a call back from the Tennessee tourism board he'd tried to get in touch with?

He answered absentmindedly, still staring at his notepad. "Evan here."

"Evan!" It was unmistakably his sister, Gina. "Oh my God, you're alive."

"Um. Shouldn't I be?"

"You've just dropped off the face of the Earth, and then we find out from *Monty*... oh, Mom's gonna kill you."

"Uh." Evan blinked and closed the notepad, trying to refocus his thoughts on something other than the new job. "She is?"

"Monty had your stuff sent here." Gina's voice grew a little more sympathetic. "Why didn't you tell us? Mom thought you'd crawled off to go die of a broken heart somewhere in Tennessee. You're not still there, are you? It's been a week and a half! Weren't you only there for a week?"

"Um." Evan's tone was distinctly guilty. "I'm staying."

"What?! Why?" she exclaimed.

He could tell his big sister anything. But he didn't want to tell her this. *I'm having a rebound while I get away from my life for a bit* just sounded... wrong.

"I'm driving down to get you," Gina told him firmly when he didn't answer for a moment.

"No, no," Evan hastened to cut her off. "No, don't. No need."

"Evan, hon, are you having a... a *moment*?"

"I haven't shaved off all my hair or joined a cult. Or even bought a sports car," Evan told her with a sigh. "Maybe I should have. Sorry. Is it a lot of stuff to store?"

"Store?"

"For a couple months. I'm staying down here until Christmas."

"Okaaay." From that tone, Evan knew he had ten seconds to explain it in a way that made her put the car keys down.

"The owner of the ranch, Josh, heard about my situation. He needed marketing help. I want to get back into the business—obviously I'm not working for Monty anymore. And he's kind. The kindest guy I've met since moving to New York."

"Right. And you're going to live in Tennessee? *You?*"

Evan mumbled, "It's actually kind of nice. Warm and friendly."

"Especially this ranch owner. You're not the type to just work on a *ranch*."

Conveniently omitting his first day of work, Evan muttered, "I'm not working *on* the ranch, really. It just needs more publicity. A marketing plan. I can help with that."

"I'm still not sure you're not having a moment, Evan," Gina told him, but her voice was kind. Somehow, that was even more annoying. "Why aren't you coming home?"

"I don't think Vermont is home for me now," Evan told her. He stood up to pace the living room of the little farmhouse. "It hasn't been since I moved away for college. But New York was only ever… well, because Monty wanted us to move in."

"Jesus. I could have ripped the bastard a new one. Good thing he sent your boxes by delivery and not himself—not that he would have *deigned* to visit us *commoners*…" Gina's venomously protective side made Evan smile.

God, it was good to talk to her again. It felt a bit more normal. He'd talked to her less and less over the years, and he hadn't realized it until now. "It's all right," Evan told her. "Really. I'm glad to be rid of him."

"Really? But you guys were fucking engaged last week, little bro."

Evan sighed. "Yeah, but before that… when he proposed, I kind of hoped that meant he was ready to fix everything. Or that it'd magically get better because we were committed, or whatever."

"I had no idea." Gina groaned. "I even congratulated you on Facebook."

"Gina," Evan laughed. "Don't beat yourself up over it."

"No, I should have seen what an asshole he was. Or told you, anyway. I never liked him."

Evan laughed as he sat on the couch again, sprawling along it and plumping a pillow behind his head. "Yeah. I ignored a lot of warning signs, to be honest."

"Feel free to tell me to mind my own business," Gina said, "but why did he dump you?"

Evan snorted. "Basically, he said I was mooching off him. That I'd been living off him for years, not working unpaid for his company—I thought it was for our future, but that was stupid. I didn't have a contract. He made me sign one after the breakup though."

"He what? Okay, fuck him. I'm going to drive down there myself," Gina fumed. "Jesus."

"No. He's not worth it."

"I think I'm supposed to be telling *you* that," Gina muttered, then laughed. "Fine. If you're gonna be all sudden Zen Evan about it, so will I. Are you really happier now?"

"I really am." A smile crept over Evan's face. "I mean, he'd been treating me like shit for a while. Nothing big, but lots of subtle things. Now I'm free to do whatever the hell I want. I don't think I want to go back to a big ad company."

The rewards—financial and personal—of hitting a deadline or nailing a creative concept had been addictive, but

Evan remembered the stress well. Getting to walk away and chase Monty's promise of a future together had been a blessing. He still remembered packing up his desk at work. Best day ever. He'd be stupid to throw himself back in that shark tank.

Especially when he had such a good thing going here.

"You did seem happier after you left…" Gina trailed off, sounding uncertain. "But then Monty happened."

"Fucking Monty," Evan grumbled.

Gina sighed. "So I guess you don't want me driving down and disturbing your peace."

"I do want to see you," Evan told her. "But not just yet. Let me figure out myself first, and I'll come home for a visit one long weekend. Maybe for Christmas or Thanksgiving."

He fought off the gnawing feeling of guilt, or perhaps even shame. It wasn't like he was hiding anything. He wasn't even really together with Josh—there was nothing to hide. But Josh deserved better than everyone thinking he was just some rebound.

"Okay, fine. Are you really, really okay?"

Every day, Evan grew more certain that the answer was yes. With Josh around, he would be.

God. If they'd met in any other circumstance, or before he'd known Monty, he would have approached it so differently. The attraction that pulled him toward Josh was magnetic, and so damn difficult to resist. Like the moment he'd seen Josh, he'd glimpsed a future. *Their* future.

But Evan didn't trust himself now. Not even to know his own heart, when he was mired in confusion and disappointment. What if Josh was just the branch he was clinging to as he pulled himself out of the swamp? What if the romance wore off and revealed nothing more than a hookup that went on for too long?

What if that was all Monty had been, ultimately, and he was afraid of that happening to him again? Trusting his gut instinct had led him right into the trap with Monty for years on end. He couldn't waste even more years with someone on no more than *but it felt right.*

Whoa. Evan's stomach lurched, and he tried to ignore the sensation. The truth had a bitter sting on his tongue, like licking a nine-volt battery.

"Yeah," Evan finally said. "I'm okay. I will be. I'm learning to be."

"Sometimes that's all we can do," Gina told him. "Okay. I'll let Mom know you're okay and you've become a hermit. Call me before you shave your head, though, babe."

Evan laughed richly. God, he was glad he had a cool family. Especially in contrast to the snippets he'd heard from Josh, who still seemed to be overcoming a bumpy start. "Thanks, Gee."

"Call Mom!" she added before she hung up.

Evan chuckled and pocketed his phone, then stretched along the sofa. It felt like home here, even if he'd been living in Josh's house for less than a week. Maybe that was because he always felt safe here.

The front door banged open.

"I'm bringing sexy back!" announced Josh as he swept into the living room with a broad grin. As usual, he was dusty and a little muddy, but his grin was infectious.

"Did it leave? How naughty." Evan pushed himself to sit upright as he smiled over at Josh. "I have some work stuff to go over with you, but you look like you'd rather hit the shower."

"Is that a hint? You're not into filthy, muddy sex?" Josh pouted.

"When you put it like that, I might be into it. But I like you squeaky-clean, too." Evan couldn't decide which he preferred right now, but he *was* wearing a clean shirt.

Josh harrumphed. "Fine. If you're trying to drop a subtle hint, I can take it."

"I can always join you, if you're so reluctant. Make sure you scrub behind your ears." Evan tried to keep his tone casual and light and flirty.

That was a thing hookups did, too, right? Shower together? You didn't have to be committed partners to learn to share the water?

"Deal." Josh stretched out his hand and crooked a finger. "Come."

"Yep." Evan shoved his laptop and notebook aside, pens falling to the floor as he abandoned the whole work setup to follow Josh's order. He took Josh's hand, and warmth flowed through him.

His skin prickled with anticipation. Whatever the hell he told himself when Josh wasn't around, it was impossible to ignore the attraction when he was.

"Kiss me," Josh murmured in that same firm, commanding tone.

Evan draped his arms lightly over Josh's shoulders, conscious that his shirt sleeves might get muddy. Had Josh been rolling in the hay?

The small, ugly, jealous part of him added: *With Kev?*

Jesus, he needed to knock it off. He didn't own the guy, nor did he have any claim to his heart. He'd specifically avoided staking that claim. If Josh wanted more—wanted a future with someone—he wasn't gonna stand in the way.

Or was he?

Evan grabbed the back of Josh's head with one hand, his other finding a spot between his shoulder blades so he could pull him in.

Josh made a startled sound but stepped forward when Evan hauled him in, their lips crashing together in a not altogether peaceful way. Whatever feelings Evan had about Kev, they were only holding an uncomfortable magnifying glass to his feelings for Josh.

I do want him. Am I going to fight for him, though? Christ, this is all so sudden!

Evan's hold tightened as he sucked Josh's lower lip and ground against him slowly, no longer caring how dirty he got. It wasn't like he needed to impress anyone with more money than sense around here. He had the feeling Josh didn't own anything dry clean-only.

"Fuck," Josh panted when Evan took a second to breathe. "What's got into you? Or hasn't, I should say."

"Your cock in my mouth. That's all I want." Evan kissed Josh's neck, unbuttoning his shirt so he could keep pressing his nose and lips along bare skin, nuzzling his way down to his chest. He kissed at Josh's nipples as he finished pulling his shirt off. Josh smelled like hard work and fresh-cut grass and desire itself.

Better yet, his cock was hard and pressing into him, and that alone was tempting enough to make him want to skip the shower. But he also wanted to tease Josh and draw out their time together so it wasn't the frantic clamor and rush toward orgasm that it usually seemed to be.

Not that there was anything wrong with hard, fast, and desperate, but Evan kind of wanted something else tonight. Something more fun.

Teasing Josh, perhaps. Seeing what kind of pressure he liked, and where on his body he liked it. Learning to play him like a finely-tuned piano.

The very idea of having Josh slick and naked under his hands was a thrill.

"About that shower," Josh drawled, and Evan couldn't help blushing. Even though it was damn obvious when Josh was teasing him, he never could help himself. But at the end of the day, Josh made him happy, and he wanted to return the favor.

"Get going," Evan told him, smacking his ass. He laughed at the surprise that flashed through Josh's eyes, and the way his lips parted into an "o" shape for a second.

Then, Josh laughed. "Cheeky!" His voice was delighted. He turned on his heel and sashayed for the bathroom, making a big deal of swinging his hips so his ass drew Evan's gaze.

"It's totally your fault," Evan informed Josh, scampering after him to squeeze his ass again and laughing as Josh broke into a trot to evade him.

They nearly fell into the bathroom together, both out of breath and laughing. Logically, it wasn't even anything terribly funny, but Evan laughed anyway, because his heart was light and the future seemed bright all of a sudden.

By the time he was on his knees in front of Josh in the shower, it was all he could do not to smile too hard to suck cock.

Every other stress just vanished when they were... fucking? Making love? Having sex? None of those words seemed to capture the spirit between them.

His last couple of weeks had been so different from any other life he'd known, but he was already hooked. Maybe a relationship could fall into place. Sex could be fun with Josh.

Not just that, but life itself was fun with Josh by his side.

CHAPTER
Eighteen

JOSH

"There's been an accident."

Josh swore and pushed himself back from his desk. His mind already jumped to the worst: how bad was it? "Where?"

"A mile up the Burr trail." Julio poked a thumb toward the door. "Bucky's saddled up in the barn. I was about to lead the next ride along the Burr too."

"Take 'em south," Josh directed. "Watch for those brambles we haven't cut back. Tanya gets spooked around them, so take the trail that cuts around the creek."

Julio saluted with two fingers and hurried off.

It took next to no time to get Heck ready. Heck, short for Heracles, had been his favorite for a couple years now. Too strong-willed for most new riders, the trail guides and Josh were the only people he usually liked. He'd put up with Evan sharing the saddle, but he made it clear he expected extra oats for it.

"Hey, boy. Ready for a run?" Josh stroked his nose as he led him out of the barn. He tried to keep his energy calm, but Heck could sense the urgency and danced sideways. "Yeah, you're ready." Josh patted his flank, then swung himself up into the saddle in one smooth motion.

Almost without prompting, as if knowing where they were going, Heck took off for the Burr trail.

It was a quick ride there, but Josh still managed to cover the range of possibilities for what he was about to see. He hadn't heard any ambulances yet, at least. Hopefully it was just a few bruises and some tears.

Heck slowed when they reached the cluster of people and horses milling around near a bend in the trail. One of the hands, Finn, was already talking with them, no doubt keeping them distracted while Kathy handled the injured guest.

Josh smiled and nodded at everyone he passed as Heck stepped around the group. "Finn, hey." What he meant was *thank you for the crowd control.*

Finn jerked his chin at Josh, then carried on telling the riveting old legend of the creek—something Kathy usually told guests. He'd been studying and listening in, then. Good. Josh liked that kind of ambition.

Crap. There was a guy on the ground, and Kathy was braced with her knees on either side of his head, holding his head still. That meant potential neck injury.

Kathy didn't look happy. Something else was going on.

Josh dismounted and strode over to them. "Hey, Kath. Hello, Mr. Smith. What happened?"

The Smiths had been a thorn in his side all week. Josh wasn't sure if he was glad it hadn't happened to someone nicer, or frustrated that there was no way he was avoiding a lawsuit now.

"Your nag threw me!" Mr. Smith nearly bellowed at him, jolting upright to glare at Josh.

"Sir, keep your neck in place until the EMTs arrive," Kathy insisted, pressing on his shoulder.

Josh crouched by him and frowned. "Which one?"

"Mona," Kathy murmured, shooting him a look of clear disbelief.

Josh didn't believe that for a second. She wouldn't even react when little kids kicked her in the sides. How Mr. Smith had gotten her to throw him, he didn't want to know.

Mona stood nearby, grazing placidly on the tall grass near the creek. Josh looked her over for any sign of injury, and Kathy shook her head. "Finn had a look and she's fine."

"Of course she's fine. It's not her goddamn neck on the line," Mr. Smith growled. "You'll be hearing about this, I can assure you. And your insurance is paying for my injuries."

Just like that, Josh's stress melted away. If this were the real deal, the insurance investigators would know. If not... well, he had nothing to worry about.

"Yes. My liability insurance will be on the job," Josh assured him. "Hold still. You don't want to make things worse. What hurts?"

"Neck and shoulders. And my back. And my goddamn rump."

Josh glanced quickly at Kathy again. "Did you see what made her throw him?"

"Nope," Kathy said. "Mona was hanging back—like she always does. Next thing I know, he's hollering. I turned around and rode back here, and he was just like this."

"Probably a goddamn butterfly," Mr. Smith blustered. "Or she saw a shadow. Your little *farm* should be shut down, you know. Dangerous for visitors. Very dangerous."

Josh didn't appreciate the condescension in his voice, but he didn't take the bait. "The investigation will turn up any failure in our duty, sir," he told him. "The liability waiver you signed—"

"I never signed no goddamn papers."

Josh sighed. He'd have to get reception to sort through the paperwork, but Ryanna was thorough. She never missed any papers. Guests often conveniently forgot they'd signed things. "Of course. We'll look at everything. First priority is getting you to the hospital."

As if on cue, the EMTs arrived. Josh didn't envy them having to immobilize him in a full-body brace and carry him a mile across the trail, with him no doubt complaining the whole way.

When he greeted the EMTs and thanked them, one of them said their ambulance was parked a little closer than the ranch. The trail forked nearby, and they'd parked about half a mile away down one of those trails.

"Where are Mrs. Smith and the kids?" he asked as they worked to strap him on the stretcher. Kathy was finally free of her duty to immobilize him, and she looked glad.

"Didn't come. Thank God. Who knows what could have happened?"

Josh bit back his irritation once more. They'd never had anything this serious happen before. Sure, there was a first time for everything, but... Mona acting out? It stretched believability. "I'll send word to them to meet you at the hospital."

For now, he had damage control to do.

"The rest of the group's a little spooked," Kathy murmured, leading him away. "But nobody saw or heard anything before this happened."

Josh raised a brow and glanced toward the EMTs, then Kathy. "Surely they won't find anything."

"Dunno. It's pretty hard to fall on purpose," Kathy pointed out. "But we can't exactly say he's making it up, can we?"

Josh sighed. "Not until we know more."

"Right. So I'll go apologize for the unforeseen circumstances," Kathy murmured.

Josh shook his head. "Nah. That's my job." When he could take the fall, he did it. It was his job, as far as he was concerned.

He dusted off his knees and headed around the bend, Kathy at his side. "Okay, folks." He got their attention instantly. "Mr. Smith is stable and headed to the hospital to check for concussions. No broken bones or anything serious as far as we can see. My apologies for the interruption to your day. Kathy's free to lead you on, or if you'd rather turn around, you can follow me back to the barn."

Murmurs went around as people looked at each other and conferred in whispers about what they'd rather do.

Josh gave them a minute before he scrambled onto Heck, patting his neck and rubbing that spot he loved to keep him calm. "Okay. Anyone heading back with me, come over this way. Everyone else, enjoy the rest of your day."

Three people did nudge their horses to approach him, looking guilty. "Sorry," one of them murmured. "I just don't feel comfortable… you know."

"Of course. Nobody should do anything they don't want to," Josh answered, even if he was fuming. "If you head back to reception, you can get a refund for the day."

Upon hearing that, a couple more people joined him, until it was a 50/50 split between those leaving and those staying on to ride longer.

"He was an annoying little man anyway," Josh distinctly

heard one woman who was staying on with Kathy murmur. It was all he could do not to laugh or agree.

He made conversation as he rode back, leading Mona alongside him. The group wasn't chatty, but at least nobody looked like they were in shock or traumatized.

Josh couldn't exactly afford all these refunds, but he'd figure out a way to make it work. There went the emergency fund for the month. Not to mention the lawyer's fees he was sure he had ahead of him.

Sure enough, by the time he left the horses in Finn's care and headed to reception, two people actually wanted to check out early. The rest just wanted refunds on the horse ride experience.

One by one, Ryanna processed them, glancing at Josh now and then.

Josh waited until the last one was gone before he let the irritated sigh slip free. He leaned on the edge of the desk and rubbed his forehead with both hands. "Why the hell did that have to happen today?"

Ryanna patted his arm. "It's an accident. It happens. It's not your fault."

"I don't think it was." Josh's lips tightened into a line. "I think he's going for an insurance payout. Not that I could let anyone overhear me say that."

"Oh, shit," she whispered. "Really?"

Josh shrugged. "Who better to find out than insurance investigators?" But it wasn't gonna help his review average in the meantime, and the autumn was already a slow time. If business dried up completely, he couldn't magically make more appear from nowhere.

Every guest paid the salaries of his employees, and he'd just taken on two more. Sure, he'd ditched the dead weight, but he'd been counting on meeting those targets. Even two people cancelling week-long vacations had a huge impact on his bottom line.

Plus, even if this was fraud and he didn't lose anything to legal fees, how was he going to publicize that and make it clear nothing had really happened? At least the waiver would cover his ass.

"Um… boss?" Ryanna sounded nervous, which was completely out of character for her.

Josh glanced quickly at her. "Yeah?"

She had a couple of file folders open on her desk with paperwork. "I can't find the waiver for Mr. Smith."

"Shit. You checked them in, didn't you?"

"Yeah. I remember I did. And I'm sure I wouldn't have missed that."

"Was he being obnoxious to distract you? Are you positive?" Josh felt dizzy. If he couldn't prove that Mr. Smith had signed it, he was about to be in deep trouble.

Ryanna shook her head quietly. "He could try that, but I'm sure I must have done it. I just don't know where the paper is."

"Fuck." Josh wouldn't swear at her, or even directly about her. He wasn't going to stoop that low. But he *was* pissed, and he had no idea how else to tell her so. All he could do now was wait for the call from his insurance company, and he could do that a lot better outside than trapped in here like a caged tiger.

He pushed himself away from the desk and strode for the door. "If anyone needs me, I'm out." He trusted them to handle the situations themselves. His cellphone was good enough, if another real emergency happened to come along today.

"And if anyone else wants refunds…?" Ryanna murmured.

"Give it to 'em. I don't care."

Despite the harsh words, Josh's heart hurt as he strode into the clear, crisp, late summer day. He did care—far too much.

Would it be so bad to lose all this headache?

If it meant losing the things he loved—cutting down fence posts to size in the wood shop, or cantering alongside a trail guide on an advanced trail ride, or showing visitors the beauty of the Tennessee mountains on a clear morning…

Or, most of all, giving people like Evan and Kev a second chance and a leg up when they needed to get back in the saddle of life? Without the ranch, how the hell was he supposed to do that?

And he'd been having the time of his life, before today. Josh pinched himself to be sure it wasn't a bad dream, but unfortunately, the sting didn't make him open his eyes to his cozy little bedroom with Evan tucked under his arm.

What the hell was he going to do?

CHAPTER

Nineteen

EVAN

Evan waited an hour longer than usual before he let himself get anxious. Josh got caught up in work some days, after all.

Surely it was easy to forget that a hot meal and a distracting pretty face waited for him at home. Or a friend with a listening ear, if that was how Josh thought of him.

Evan kind of hoped Josh went with the first option.

But when the sun crept quite a bit further down the horizon than usual and Josh still hadn't shown up, Evan figured it couldn't hurt to go retrieve him from his paper-work or fencepost-mending.

"Hey. Any sign of Josh?" he asked at the reception, giving Ryanna a friendly smile.

She frowned as she looked up from the computer. "No. He's been gone all afternoon."

Evan's heart skipped a beat. Where on Earth had he gone, then? "Where was he last?"

"Outside." On a ranch this size, that was hardly helpful.

"You could try calling," Ryanna added. "I didn't want to bother him today. I think he's with Kev, though."

Evan took that to mean that Josh was in a bad mood. If anyone was obligated to help, it was him. "Oh. Okay. Thanks," he told her and waved, digging out his phone to call Josh.

It went straight to voicemail. At least Josh wasn't ignoring him on purpose. It didn't do anything for the fear that paralyzed him now, though. What if he'd fallen somewhere and he couldn't make it to help? What if he'd…

Wait. In the distance, along the fields and in the direction of the spot where they'd identified broken fencing, he saw two figures.

One was sitting on a fence post, and the other on the ground beside him. Or kneeling beside him—they were too far away to be sure.

I'm sure he's not hooking up with Kev. Not after all we've been through together. He didn't say he wanted anyone else. But we didn't say that's off the table, either.

His own doubts had several minutes to gnaw at him as he picked his way along the field, following the fence line toward the figures. Gradually, the details became clearer: Josh leaned heavily on the post, his hands bracing himself. Kev was sitting on the ground next to him, his head almost touching Josh's legs as he leaned back against the same post.

The jealous little voice in Evan's head told him that it looked like an intimate pose—like two lovers recovering from some vigorous exertion.

Next to them was a pile of lumber and tools Evan couldn't identify—presumably for fixing the fencing, since there was a gap several fence posts wide.

Finally, one of them spotted him. Josh rose to his feet and

waited for Evan to come within earshot, looking down at Kev as they talked.

"Hey," Evan called when he finally came close enough to have a reasonable conversation. He tried to keep his focus on Josh and not the pretty boy next to him. It was completely stupid of him, but he couldn't stop himself resenting Kev for having spent the day with Josh.

Josh waved back. "Getting late. Sorry. I didn't notice."

"No, I'm sure." Evan glanced at Kev and back to Josh. "Time flies when you're having fun."

God, that came out snottier than he'd intended.

Kev pushed himself to his feet and stretched. He met Evan's gaze evenly, but his gaze betrayed nothing. He just nodded in greeting.

"Fun and hard work." Josh wiped his arm along his forehead. "You like the new look?"

Evan glanced at the fence. It was clear which posts were new, but it looked like only half of them were in place. What had he been up to for the rest of the day?

I'm such a loser. I can't even put a lid on it for ten seconds, he thought. "Yeah. It looks… new."

The silence between them stretched for a few seconds.

"Right. I'm off, then?" Kev said, glancing at Josh.

"Free to go. Thanks for your help today."

"Anytime." Kev glanced between Evan and Josh. "See you tomorrow," he told Josh then with a crooked smile. "Thanks for today."

Was he deliberately baiting Evan? Evan's temper flared. "I bet it was a good time."

"Yep." Kev's smile only grew. "You two better sort out whatever this is before tomorrow, though. I don't like being in the middle of this shit."

Evan's cheeks burned at the reprimand. Technically, he didn't have any kind of authority over Kev, and vice versa. He raised his eyebrow and bit his tongue.

"Will do," Josh said. "See you, Kev."

After the leggy blond was out of sight, Evan folded his arms tightly, trying to bring his emotions back under control. It barely worked. "You're not sleeping with him, right?"

"Whoa," Josh laughed. "That came out of nowhere."

Evan's shoulders were tight, and his breathing almost hurt. It felt like he was clinging onto something precious with his fingertips—no, just his fingernails—and the harder he held on, the less sure he was of his grip.

"No. It's sudden for you, maybe," Evan murmured, looking down at the ground. "But it's situation normal for me. Monty used to…"

He'd held on tightly to Monty, whenever he was allowed. He'd never directly brought anything up when he suspected that Monty hadn't been faithful, but he also hadn't wanted to know. Hell, that in itself was unhealthy as fuck, and he knew it.

Whenever he'd been jealous, though, it usually meant he needed something. From Monty, that was any kind of affection or romance or sexual desire. Josh showed him all of the above already. So what was this about?

God, there was no escaping it, was there?

"I know," Josh told him quietly. "But we were trying not to do a relationship. And this doesn't sound like that. This sounds like you want to be monogamous, which… *is* a relationship."

"I want something more with you." Evan was suddenly very conscious that this wasn't the best spot to talk about it

—right out here in the field, the sun setting, the frogs chirping in the distant creek. He could have waited until the dinner table, damn it.

Josh pulled Evan into his arms, but instead of kissing Evan when he turned his face expectantly toward him, Josh just hugged tightly.

Ouch. His whole body hurt for a second, like he'd been slapped. It felt like a "let's be friends" move, and his heart was suddenly on the line.

"I've had the time of my life," Josh murmured, and it took Evan a second to recognize it.

"Oh, fuck off. I'm serious." Evan tried to wriggle free, and Josh let go.

Josh was smiling at him. "So am I. You don't wanna date me, though." The way Josh said it was utterly certain, like he knew something Evan didn't.

Did he have some big, dark secret? Was he a serial killer? Did he forget anniversaries? Put ketchup on his mac and cheese?

Evan opened his mouth to protest, but Josh cut him off. "Not when I can't even run the damn business."

"What?" Evan frowned.

"I'm coming up short. Not enough coming in to pay everyone until Christmas. I'll have to stop activities a couple weeks early this year." Josh's speech was matter-of-fact and clipped. "There was a riding accident earlier. A couple people checked out early. Two more called to cancel their reservations. I don't know how word's getting out—probably social media. Anyway, long story short, money is a lot tighter all of a sudden."

Evan was used to that voice. It usually meant he was being a pain in the ass, and he should get over himself and let

Monty do more important things. He pressed his lips together and nodded. "Well, you could always not pay me."

Josh looked startled. "What?"

"I have a place to live. And I'm responsible for bringing in more business. I can work on commission if things are that bad."

Josh shook his head and chuckled. "No, Evan."

"Why not?" Evan demanded. He was sick of being treated like he wouldn't understand finances when they were actually well within his wheelhouse.

"You remember Monty, right?"

The words stung all over again. How the hell could Josh think he'd forgotten already? Unless this was a veiled criticism.

And it hit too close to home. Evan *had* known Monty was using him, on some level, but he had chosen not to believe it. So it was his own damn fault Monty had taken advantage of him, really. Josh was right about that.

The part that scared him more was that maybe Josh thought this was short-term, too. No wonder Josh didn't want to commit to anything.

He'd sidestepped the question earlier. Not even by having the guts to say he didn't want to date Evan, but that Evan shouldn't want to date him.

Frustration knotted in his chest and pricked at the corners of his eyes. Evan refused to let Josh see him upset, though. He'd done quite enough crying on his shoulder, thank you very much.

He turned on his heel and set off along the fence, back to Josh's house. He hoped he'd calm down by the time he got there, but he doubted it.

In any case, his appetite was gone.

Twenty

JOSH

WELL, IF JOSH HADN'T FELT LIKE SHIT BEFORE, HE SURE DID now. He wasn't even sure what he'd done wrong. There were too many possibilities to choose from.

Should he have made it clear that he and Kev weren't an item? He'd thought that was obvious from the last few weeks of courting Evan.

Should he have told Evan properly why he was so stressed out and finding it hard to have meaningful relationship conversations?

Should he have let Evan know that he was trying to hitch his wagon to what could easily become a lost cause, if he couldn't dig up any more proof that Mr. Smith was a lying asshole?

But of course it was Monty who had been the last straw. Even mentioning his name had upset Evan. And when Josh thought about it, the way he'd mentioned him *had* been cold.

Well done, dumbass. There were a million ways he could have explained himself better.

Josh wasn't used to shattering conversations with careless words. Ever since he'd escaped here—escaped his dad —he'd sworn not to use his words to cut people down. Only to build them up. Whenever he joked about things with his friends, he made damn sure they knew he was only teasing.

He'd failed to do that here, and he felt like a big, stupid failure.

Josh slid down the post to sit on the grass for a minute, pulling his arms around his knees and burying his face in them. It was a position he'd sat in before, as a kid. When the shouting got to be too much for him, he'd retreat inward and press his face into his knees until fireworks of sparks erupted behind his eyes.

But he wasn't a kid anymore. His hands might be shaky and his heart might be racing at the very idea of figuring out what he'd done wrong and fixing it, but he had the power here.

He owned the goddamn place. So why did it feel like he was still accountable to some invisible boss who wouldn't let him eat supper?

He rubbed his eyes with his fist for a moment and took a deep breath, rolling his head back against the fence post to look up at the sky.

Shades of pink and red stretched across the horizon in bands of gloriously vivid color. The sun was golden and dipping fast. It was clearly almost autumn, because as it did so, a hint of a chill crept into the air. No more of those cool, relaxing summer evenings for a little while.

Frankly, the heat and the height of summer got old in a hurry. The change was a good thing. Another winter to relax and sort his shit out meant next summer would be glorious.

If he made it that long.

Josh dug his phone out of his pocket and sent a text, ignoring the missed call notifications.

Hey guys. A little advice?

Without waiting for a reply from any of his good friends, he elaborated on the problem.

I like this guy a lot. And I just said something stupid. I feel like he's going to come tell me off.

The first one to answer was Tyler, which made him smile.

Dude, he's sweet as a button. He's not gonna tear you a new one for saying something stupid. ... How stupid tho?

Josh grinned. *A little dumb. I rubbed in his ex at the wrong moment.*

Ouch. That was Blane. *Flowers work well.*

Abruptly, Josh recoiled. He wasn't even sure why his chest was so tight for a few moments, until the memory hit him with every vivid ounce of emotion he'd felt at the time.

He'd skipped chores one day when he was about nine. Ran out to sit under a tree with the GameBoy he'd borrowed off a kid in school. He'd spent a perfectly lazy afternoon there—perfect except for the ever-present fear of being found. Somehow, though, the knowledge his dad wasn't bothering to look for him was even worse.

When he'd finally had to go inside, he'd known perfectly well he wouldn't get supper. He'd tried bringing flowers from the field into the house for his dad, to soften the blow.

His dad had ripped them from his hands and thrown them on the ground.

Don't be such a fucking pussy, Josh. Stand there and take it like a man.

So, tears brimming in his eyes, he'd stood there and listened as Dad told him how he was letting down the family, and how his mom would be disappointed if she only knew.

And then he'd gone outside and worked in the barn until midnight, until his eyes wouldn't stay open anymore.

His dad had carried him inside and put him to bed—he just remembered opening his eyes when his dad pulled the covers up around his shoulders.

I'm sorry, Dad had murmured. *I don't know what I'm doing. I wish you were here, Linda.* That was his mom, whose name he rarely spoke. Then, despite this rare moment of vulnerability, he'd been too tired to listen in anymore.

Josh wiped his face again, grimacing at the wetness there. He had to get over himself and all that shit someday. But the more he told himself that, the less it seemed to work.

He picked up his phone again.

I never told you guys something. My dad used to yell at me a lot. The sleepovers and gaming nights I missed, it was because he didn't let me leave without doing chores. Sometimes eat. There was a lot of stuff I never said.

Josh's hands shook as he hit Send.

The responses were instant: hugs, heart emoticons, and in Tyler's case, *I knew he was an asshole bc you never invited us over. But I didn't know how bad. Strong + silent isn't always good you know.*

Josh blinked, still feeling shaky as he answered. *I thought I was being too sensitive or whatever.*

You're worried Evan will yell at you for saying something dumb? That was Dustin. *That's a pretty clear sign your dad took it too far and you got hurt. I'm sorry we didn't know or we could have helped.*

So was Josh. He'd give anything to turn back time and have some other way out, but he'd taken the only way he'd seen at the time: sinking himself into the work his dad gave him, using school to escape.

Now go find that man and say you're sorry. Tell him why you're afraid of fucking up with him. Blane's advice was solid as ever.

In for a penny, in for a pound. *Do I love him? Is that dumb?? It's too soon. It's been like 2 weeks.* Josh pushed himself upright to lean on the fence again, his breathing quick. Admitting it —even in texts—seemed like it would make him vulnerable.

But he was tired of keeping secrets. He wasn't going to let this be something else he'd later regret not asking for help with.

The responses flooded in moments later:

Blane: *It's never too soon. If your heart says yes, then follow it.*

Alec: *I knew the moment I saw him.*

Roman: *I knew the moment I slept with him.*

Oscar: *Ditto ;)*

Nico: *Didn't want to know that. But I knew when I didn't want to let Deen leave. It was like a flashing sign pointed to him and said he's the one.*

Deen: *When the whole "you'll know when you meet the one" makes sense but it still scares the shit out of you.*

Josh took a deep breath and nodded to himself. He knew what he had to do. He was trembling, but bravery wasn't about feeling no fear. It was about doing the right thing, even if you were shaking in your boots.

Thanks, guys. BRB.

The walk to the house was brisk, because Josh wasn't giving himself a moment to think twice about it. They were right, and he wasn't going to let this slip out of his fingers.

He pushed open the front door and kicked his shoes off,

shrugging off his overshirt to leave it and its dust in the hallway.

"Evan?" he called, not letting himself sneak inside. He needed to have this conversation now.

Evan was in the living room, curled up on the couch. He pushed himself upright, sluggish to respond and wary but offering a tiny, tentative smile. "Yeah?"

"I'm sorry I said something stupid." Josh's steps slowed as he approached Evan, then sat on the couch next to him and put a hand on his thigh. "I didn't want to hurt you. I didn't really think about what I said first."

It took all his courage to make that move, to say those words. Maybe Evan saw a hint of it in his expression, because his gaze softened, and then he took Josh's hand.

"I know you didn't mean it the way I took it. I just couldn't help it, either. It seemed like you were..." he hesitated, his head dropping as if he were a little afraid to say it.

Josh nodded. "Criticizing you, not him?"

"Yeah." Evan pushed his hair around, still avoiding Josh's gaze.

Josh nodded. "I meant it as a criticism against myself. I like what we've got going on. I don't want to fuck it up. Whether that's by saying something stupid, or by taking advantage of you like he did."

Understanding finally blossomed over Evan's face, and he sat up a little straighter. "Oh. Right. You didn't mean that I'm an idiot."

Josh grabbed Evan's hand. "No. God, no." He didn't know how else to emphasize his words, so he squeezed tightly. "It's not your fault when someone else treats you badly."

After a few moments, softly, Evan asked, "Did anyone ever say that to you?"

It hit Josh like a cartoon frying pan to the face. He reeled for a few moments, lips parting and then closing tightly again before he could come up with a response. He just shook his head.

"They should have." Evan scooted closer to him, his arm slipping around Josh's shoulders. "I'm not going to yell at you for saying something dumb. You look like a deer in the headlights."

Josh felt his cheeks flush with heat. "I do?" When Evan nodded, he cleared his throat. "Ah. Yeah. Well." He couldn't very well avoid saying it, though. Not with Evan looking expectantly at him. "It was still my fault for being dumb sometimes."

A strange fierceness in his eyes, Evan glared at him. "No."

"No?" Josh wasn't sure what to make of this reaction, and he held still. It felt like he was waiting to see if Evan would bite, or yell at him.

And then, abruptly, he realized that this was exactly what Evan meant. The air left his lungs in a quick rush.

"Oh."

Evan hugged Josh, and Josh found his head resting on his shoulder as they cradled each other. For a few weeks now, Josh had seen himself as taking care of Evan—and he didn't think that had been completely wrong. But suddenly, Josh realized that Evan wasn't the only one being taken care of right now.

"He didn't like talking things out," Josh muttered. "Only reason I came to talk to you now was... well, my brothers. I've learned better from them."

Evan rubbed his back and nodded, but said nothing.

To fill the silence, Josh kept talking. The words suddenly wouldn't stop. "It wasn't like he hurt me. He never smacked me around, you know? I would've known that was wrong. It was subtler. He used to make me skip meals if I skipped chores. Wouldn't let me back in the house if I snuck out as a teen. That kind of stuff. Stuff that seems like good character-building, but just makes you think you don't have anywhere safe, and you're not allowed to fuck up, and you're going to turn out a fuck-up no matter what you do."

Evan's hands rubbed gentle circles along his shoulder blades, down his back, and up to the back of his neck again. He still said nothing, but his hold was a little tighter.

"I finally told my brothers. Just now." Josh sighed, the tension draining from him at Evan's quiet acceptance. Evan wasn't getting mad or judging or anything. He was just here, listening. "I don't know why I waited so long. So…" he trailed off, running out of things to say.

"Good," Evan murmured, finally breaking his silence. "You deserve support. It doesn't have to pass some test of how bad it is before it can affect you. And pushing me away won't work."

Josh felt raw and vulnerable, but Evan was being gentle. "Oh. I… I really appreciate that," he said slowly. It was too soon to tell Evan that he saw a future with him, and he both loved that fact and was scared shitless at the same time.

"Next time you lash out first, I'll hand you your ego on a platter." Evan patted Josh's thigh and winked. "This was your one get-out-of-jail-free card."

Reality came sneaking back in, as much as Josh wanted to sit here all evening and talk to Evan. "I need to unmute my phone. I just… took a break from reality there. But the lawyers… and insurance… and… God. I don't know. Will the cops get involved?"

"Tell me about the accident." Evan's voice was firm and confident, and Josh couldn't have appreciated it more.

When he needed a shoulder, he'd always had one to turn to—but he'd never let himself do so for too long.

Something about his stubborn independence had to change if he wanted to keep this man around and not fuck up like this again.

Just when everything felt like it was settling into place, too.

But if he had Evan by his side, who was willing to give him another chance and listen and not be a dick just because Josh had made a mistake… well, he suddenly felt safer with Evan.

Maybe the rewards of vulnerability were worth the risk.

CHAPTER

Twenty-One

JOSH

THE LETTER WAS EXACTLY AS INTIMIDATING AS HE'D EXPECTED. Heavy paper weight, fancy font for the lawyer's office name, and two-dollar words all over it.

"That the asshole's spurious letter?" Evan had spotted the envelope before him, and he was perched on the edge of the desk, his expression anxious.

"I'm not sure what spurious means, but I'm pretty sure he ain't gay. Spurting letters are off the table for him."

Evan snorted. "Threadbare, then. Full of lies. In a wrapper of lies."

"Oh. Yeah, it's his lies. Blah blah, covering his medical bills, negligence, all that shit. They're asking for…" Josh trailed off at the amount of money. Eighty grand? "Are you fucking kidding? I can't pay that."

Evan shook his head. "You shouldn't pay the asshole a dime."

Josh grimaced. "So, hire a lawyer and waste money that way?"

"Are you sure Ryanna didn't forget the paperwork?"

Josh spun in his office chair, looking around at the old maps and photos he knew like the back of his hand. It was hard to put faith in people, but his people were good. He trusted them. More than his dad had ever done with his hired help—and they rose to the demands Josh made because of it, he was sure. People needed to be trusted.

Not that he'd been thinking about Evan and their arrangement way too much lately.

"Yeah. I'm sure."

"Right." Evan looked all business. "So task one: find out what happened. Task two: see if anyone has dirt on this accident. Task three: get a lawyer to fend off this one for a while."

"Are you my new manager? I think I might love you," Josh said. He tried his goddamn hardest to make it sound light and teasing and joking.

Just to test the waters.

Evan's eyes flickered quickly to him, and then he smirked. "I am. I'm good at keeping people on task. Oh, and the horse."

"We can't interview Mona," Josh said with a grin.

"No," Evan murmured. He was gazing into the distance, too distracted to get the joke. "But we can put a newbie on her and have him annoy her and see if she reacts. There were no injuries on her, so he can't have done anything serious that would be wrong to try out. Just tugging the reins and that kind of stuff."

"She won't react." Josh was confident in that. Even the fidgety or bratty kids couldn't get her to disrupt her mellow mood. "But she trusts all of us too much. She wouldn't react like she did to him, unless she was with someone…" He spotted the gleam in Evan's eye. "No."

"You just said it wasn't a risk."

Josh pressed his lips together to stop the smile. The jerk

was right. "It'd be a waste of time though. She's never acted like this at all." To keep Evan from looking disappointed at his idea falling through, he added, "Better you focus on something else."

"Okay. I'll handle the lawyer."

Josh blinked. "You know lawyers?" The moment it came out of his mouth, he winced. *Of course he does, dumbass. He got a fucking contract from one when he broke up.* "That I can afford?" he added quickly, hoping to save the moment.

Evan gave him a crooked smile, no doubt noticing the slip. "Yeah. A couple of them owe me favors now. Monty might be an asshole, but his friends aren't. Well, not all of them."

Josh sucked in a breath. The last thing he wanted to do was force Evan to relive his very recent past. "I can't ask you—"

"Of course you can't. You didn't ask." Evan gave him a look that Josh could tell meant *no arguments.*

Josh opened his mouth, then closed it again. He was smart enough to know when he'd lost. "I guess I'll see about tracking down that waiver."

"Good call." Evan winked and patted his shoulder, then snapped a photo of the letter. "I'll need to email it over to some people. Back in a bit."

"Do what you need to." Josh looked around the office as Evan hurried out, then rubbed his head. He hadn't even thought about it, but Mr. Smith had only checked in a week ago. CCTV didn't keep footage that long, but it gave him an idea.

What if the waiver *had* been signed? The cabinet with those papers was kept locked, but if you knew that the keys were in the desk drawer, you could get in. So if Mr. Smith had help…

Like a bolt out of the blue, the thought hit him: Adam.

No way. He never knew crap about the office, did he? But then, he'd been in here for lunch breaks sometimes. He had as much chance of seeing something as anyone.

But why the hell would he sabotage anything?

"Ryanna?" He strode out of the office. "Can you check the paperwork for everyone who checked in around the same time?"

Ryanna didn't need to ask what he meant—she grabbed the keys and got to work. "Thinking it might not be just his that went missing?"

Josh bit his thumbnail and paced. "I don't know. If it is just him…" he trailed off, lost in thought. How much of a coincidence was that? Too much. Coincidences didn't exist, in his mind.

"Huh. Just his," Ryanna said. "I've checked a day before and after. Everything else is in place. But the papers were out of order in his folder."

"Really." It wasn't a question. He'd had some suspicion that would be the case. And all signs pointed to someone tampering with the paperwork, then.

"Right. So you're thinking someone… who?" Ryanna squinted at him. "I mean, we've never needed to keep track of the keys closely."

"Anyone could wait for you to step away between checkout and checkin time for a break, right?" Josh murmured to himself. "When did you last see Adam?"

Ryanna hissed through clenched teeth. "Day after you fired him. I came out and he was just leaving. Turned around, said he wanted to say goodbye. But he could have…" she trailed off, her brows raising.

"Would he have had time?"

"Yeah. He could have." Ryanna winced. "God, I'm sorry, boss. I would've eaten at my desk…"

Josh shook his head. "You weren't supposed to know. I'm just trying to figure out what he's playing at. If he knew something would happen… did he spook Mona?"

"That don't seem likely." When Josh shot Ryanna a questioning look, she shrugged. "Everyone knows Mona's the least spookable beast around, including us. I think there could be an earthquake under her feet and she'd just sigh and move on to the next tuft of grass."

Josh chuckled. "Yeah. So how'd he know something was…" he trailed off. *Of course,* he thought. How could he have been so dumb? He hadn't had an accident at all. "I need to talk to my insurance people."

"You sure do." Ryanna had a steely glint in her eye. "If you really think it was Adam's work, I'll give him a swift kick up the ass."

The door rattled and Josh turned to it, half-expecting Adam to be standing there, preparing a villain's monologue to explain why he'd done it.

But it was a pretty blond woman wearing a long ponytail through a baseball cap, standing a full head shorter than him. She wore bright pink high heels and a scowl. She looked vaguely familiar, but Josh didn't have time to place her before she strode up to him.

"You Josh, the owner here?" Her accent was distinctly not local.

"Yeah, that's me."

"So it's your ass I'll have to kick."

"Uh…"

Josh blinked, trying to figure out what he'd done wrong now. It was getting hard to keep track of his unexpected enemies. He must have been a real bastard in a past life.

In any case, he moved his hand slightly toward the family jewels, ready to take shelter if he had to. Those heels looked deadly. He finally dared to ask the first of many questions that came to mind.

"Why?"

"Mom's pretty sure my brother's lost his mind and joined some dude ranch cult."

Once he'd processed that sentence, it took all Josh had not to burst out laughing. "You're… are you related to… who's your brother?"

She eyed him. "You have a lot of new recruits?"

"You'd be surprised." She looked like Evan now that he was thinking about it. Way more than Kev. But he couldn't be too sure, and if Kev was hiding out from his family, he wasn't going to reveal his presence.

"Evan. Yea high," she held up a hand at around his height, "brown eyes, insufferably preppy fashion sense."

Josh *did* let a snicker escape, despite his best efforts. He clapped a hand over his mouth at the look she gave him. "Um. Yeah, he's here."

"What about Monty? Do you know who Monty is? Is he here?"

Do I ever, Josh thought ruefully. "Unfortunately, I do, and no. He got to his car before I could."

She hummed. "I see we share the same feeling about Monty." He couldn't believe the similarity to Evan when this woman got down to business. The same efficiency, practicality, and no-nonsense attitude. "We might not be enemies, then," she decided.

"Enemy of your enemy is your friend?" Josh offered. "He left a couple weeks ago. I'd have kicked his ass into the Pacific if he'd tried to come back."

"Depends if the enemy of my enemy has coffee." She peeled her baseball cap off and shook her ponytail free, finally relaxing her stance and the fist on her hip. "I could murder for a good cup."

Ryanna was already moving for the coffee maker, looking for all the world like she was trying not to laugh. This was gonna be the talk of the ranch for days.

"Of course. Have a seat. Did you drive?"

"From Vermont."

Josh's jaw dropped. "Oh, shit. Seriously, have a seat." He ushered her toward the chairs tucked in the corner and took a seat himself.

"I've been sitting enough damn hours," she sighed. "I need to pace." She didn't even wobble as she strode over to Ryanna to accept the cup of coffee, and she gave a grateful sigh as she chugged it. "Oh, God. That's amazing. Elixir of life."

"That must be, like, a twelve-hour drive." Josh glanced at the clock—it was definitely morning. Had she driven overnight?

"Oh, I stopped in Roanoke. I had an ex-boyfriend who was thrilled to see me." She grinned. "He regrets the ex-girlfriend after me a lot more now."

Josh burst out laughing for real this time. She was everything Evan wasn't, yet he could see more of Evan in her now that Evan was opening up every day. Not that much confidence yet, but the wicked sense of humor and playful attitude. "Did you come all this way because you really thought he's in a cult?"

"Hey, I don't know better. Seems like a legit dude ranch to me, but Mom tells me to drive down to Tennessee or she won't make my favorite stuffing at Thanksgiving? I'm going to Tennessee." She put her cap on again and reached out to shake hands. "Gina."

"Josh. Though you know that already. God knows what Evan's said about me, but it's probably not true," Josh said and grinned.

"The part about you being the kindest guy he's met since moving to New York?"

Josh knew from the heat level of his cheeks that he must be turning tomato-red. He hastily stood up and dusted his hands on his jeans, clearing his throat. "Well, uh, I don't know about that. He needed a job and I had one. Speaking of which, I should walk you up to the house. I've got a guest room. Got any bags?"

"Aw, modest *and* a gentleman. One, but I'll manage it myself. I'd rather see Evan first," Gina told him and strode out the door.

Despite his concern, she managed the ranch terrain in those murderous heels, and even chatted as she did it. He was starting to like her. *The in-laws aren't so bad, it turns out. If only they were in-laws for real.* He wouldn't mind Gina as a sister-in-law.

They ran into him just coming down the path, and Josh grinned at the look on his face.

Evan looked like he wasn't sure what he was seeing with his own eyes. "Uh. I… Gina?" He rubbed his eyes.

Gina grabbed him and hauled him in for a hug, nearly

knocking him off-balance despite being a good six inches shorter than them both. "Come here, you asshole."

"Oh my God. It *is* you!" Evan recovered himself and hugged her back so tightly she squeaked. "Gee, you didn't have to… oh my God, why are you all the way down here?"

"Mom thought you were part of a cult. I wanted to meet your newer, better boyfriend." Gina's eyes sparkled mischievously as she glanced between them.

Josh's blush had only just faded, and it came back in full force the moment Evan looked at him. He cleared his throat and waved up at the house. "I, uh, offered the guest room."

A few seconds passed as both he and Gina watched Evan. Then, the lightbulb came on as he realized that having a spare room meant it was obvious the two of them were sleeping together.

Evan made a strange half-groan, half-laugh sound. "I wasn't—I mean, we're not officially…"

"Yeah, you've put on five pounds and you actually smiled at me just there." Gina clapped his shoulder. "I like this guy already. Don't make excuses. Now, show me a place I can sit down and analyze Monty's flaws one by one. Preferably with whiskey. You guys have tons of that down here, right?"

Josh choked back a laugh at Evan's expression. He still hadn't touched whiskey since the mini-bar incident. "I'll leave you two to it. I've got a man to see about a thing." Evan cast him a look of concern, and he smiled. "I think I've solved the mystery. I'll let you know how it turns out. You just relax."

"I've got you a lawyer," Evan answered before Gina could tug him toward the house. "A friend, of sorts. Free of charge. He's gonna rip that other lawyer apart for fun and giggles."

"I—" Josh stopped himself. Even a joking *I love*

you wouldn't help Evan's case if he was trying to say they weren't together. But Gina just smirked at him expectantly. "Uh… you… yeah."

"Yeah," Evan answered, his smile widening until dimples appeared in his cheeks. "Damn right you do. I *uh* you, too."

Gina snickered, and Evan joined in the laughter as Josh turned tail and fled. As he reached his car, Josh finally took a moment to lean on it and laugh. God, he felt like a moron. He couldn't even get the simplest words out, apparently.

Josh's only consolation was that Evan's interrogation was about to begin, and he didn't envy him for it. He had no doubt Gina was good at getting the dirt. And Josh had a little interrogation of his own to do in the meantime.

CHAPTER

Twenty~Two

EVAN

"I can't believe how happy you seem around here. And there are *cows*. And *horses*." Gina's gesture toward the living room wall was supposed to encompass the farm, but it looked like she was offended by the—admittedly tacky—old metal Coke plaque that hung there.

Evan had to admit that it *was* a kitschy place: horses, old advertising, and all. But there was something that drew Evan toward it, too. He couldn't put a finger on it. "I just… there's something."

"Named Josh?"

"More than that," Evan laughed. "Before I realized how well we work together. It was peaceful here. I mean, it's hard work… day in and day out… the kind of work Monty's allergic to. But there's something satisfying about that, too."

"Next thing I know you'll be barrel racing."

"Oh, shut up," Evan laughed, throwing a couch cushion at her.

Gina caught it and smacked him over the head with it,

with a solid *fwump* sound. "Don't start games with a big sister who can kick your ass," she warned.

Evan grinned. "I never did learn that."

"Good. That fighting spirit is back, too."

"Huh?"

Gina looked askance at him. "You never noticed? You were a shell of yourself around Monty."

Like he wasn't already aware that Monty was the biggest mistake of his life. Evan sighed and shook his head. "Yeah, I'm growing to realize that."

Gina put her arm around him. "I'm sorry, though. It still sucks."

After a moment, Evan relaxed and put his head on her shoulder. His big sister played rough and tumble with him, but she'd always kissed his bruises, too, and stood up for him when he got in trouble, and scared off the bullies for him.

How had he been so out of touch with everyone for so long?

"I can't let that happen again," he murmured to himself, straightening up again.

"Yeah. That's why I wanted to check on you here. Make sure you weren't jumping from the frying pan to the fire," Gina murmured. "That and Mom said she wouldn't make my stuffing at Thanksgiving. And Danny offered me a place to stay in Roanoke." She smirked.

Evan wrinkled his nose and laughed. "Really?"

"Hey. I'm not advising you to try the idea with Monty, but no-strings-attached fun is a great idea sometimes." Gina shrugged.

"Until you find the strings that were there all along." Evan folded his arms and leaned back into the couch with a sigh.

"So? You two are happy together, right? Don't overthink it," Gina told him.

"Yeah, but he's happy the way we are. Without a label."

"Are you sure?"

"He said that much."

Gina squinted at him. "You're good at jumping to conclusions when it's your heart on the line. Have you asked if he wants to be boyfriends?"

"Fucking ouch, Gee. No rest for the wicked here. Called out." Evan pretended to swoon against the cushions. "It's all too much."

"Shut up. You haven't, have you?" Gina grinned at his resigned expression. "So that's your first problem. You love him, don't you? You two almost said it. It was adorable."

Evan groaned and stayed where he was, but he hauled the cushion to cover his face and hugged it with both arms. "Fuck my life."

"You haven't said it for real, then," Gina surmised. "Right. Well, you guys are just a bundle of nerves, aren't you? You *do* love each other. It shouldn't be easy to say."

"Good. Then I'm madly, head-over-heels, completely and utterly in love with him, and I'm going to fucking die if he ever hears that."

"I better go, then." The deep voice from the hallway was nothing like Gina's.

Evan flailed with the couch cushion and rolled off the couch, hitting the floor with a solid *thump*. "Ow!"

"Shit, Evan. You're as clumsy as always." Gina clicked her tongue and glanced up at Josh, who was wearing a shit-eating grin and leaning in the doorway. "That was a little mean, but I like it. Keep him on his toes."

Evan flipped them both off and dragged the cushion over

his face again. His heart pounded, and his hands almost shook. Fuck. But Josh hadn't looked weirded out, or even like he was about to patiently turn him down. When he peeked again, Josh was still grinning at him. "Oh, you can both fuck off."

Gina laughed and stood up. "I'm gonna grab lunch. I saw a cute place in town. You guys sort things out, and then I'll be back for that guest room," she told them and strode for the hall.

Evan just grunted back at her and stayed firmly on the floor, the pillow pressed to his chest as he stared up at Josh.

When the door clicked shut, Josh wandered closer until he sat on the couch. He leaned over and tugged on the cushion as Evan tightened his hold, and only too late did Evan realize that he was trying to pull him to sit upright. It worked.

"That was really unfair," he said with a pout.

Josh chuckled, but he wrapped his arm around Evan's shoulders, too. He was leaning forward, and he pulled him closer until Evan's head pressed against his shoulder. "I'm sorry."

"No, you're not."

"A little sorry. But not completely, let alone head-over-heels."

Evan harrumphed, but it only earned him a chuckle. "What do you want, then?"

"To talk about this."

The edge in Josh's voice was barely noticeable. To anyone else, it sounded like he was still kidding around. But Evan spotted the nervousness there, too. And the tension in his body as Evan stood up and sat next to him on the couch. And the way Josh looked away, then back at Evan, his eyes darting around the room as if in search of an escape route.

"Okay," Evan murmured. He didn't want to scare Josh off, and it was now or never to talk about this stuff. "Yeah, that wasn't an ideal way of telling you, but I think I do love you. I was being a little over-the-top…"

Josh chuckled. "Yeah, I heard the context. Don't worry. I don't think you're a crazy stalker suddenly."

"Oh, thank God." Evan laughed, and Josh joined in. "But yeah, I… I felt like it was too soon to tell you."

"Because of the rebound thing?"

Evan winced. "Yeah. I didn't think you'd believe me. I mean, it *is* awfully soon."

"Your sister said you're a hell of a lot happier. I've noticed it, too. Hell, Ryanna's noticed. Everyone has."

Evan blinked in surprise. He hadn't realized everyone had been keeping such a close eye on him. "Really? I mean, I feel it, but…"

"They give a shit," Josh assured him quietly, hearing his real question. "So do I. And yeah, I love you. I don't know, maybe it *is* too soon, but there's something about you that makes me wanna hang in there and find out what that's all about."

Evan was already nodding. "Exactly." Thank God he didn't have to explain how he felt. Josh had a lot of words for his feelings, considering how ill-used to sharing them he really was. And he thought he was bad at this stuff? Yeah, right. "I just didn't know… I thought you were happy as-is."

"I am," Josh said. He gave a crooked smile. "But I thought that about you. I mean, I didn't want to pressure you into more when you should be enjoying your freedom."

Evan shook his head. "Freedom from a shitty relationship, yeah. That doesn't have to mean freedom from *all* relationships. When you find a guy who treats you like gold, even if you're at the bottom of the pit when you find him... if he can hang on long enough for you to claw your way out..."

Josh gripped his hand. "I'll be here," he murmured. "Take your time. We don't have to label it. If it's too soon, we don't even have to tell family or friends. Whenever you're ready, I'll be here."

"I know," Evan whispered, pressing his cheek against Josh's shoulder. "Which is exactly *why* I'm ready. I mean, I thought this was just a rebound, too. I thought I'd get a taste of something better, a taste of single life... but then I fell into this, and I can't walk away just because of when I found you."

"Oh." A long sigh escaped Josh's lips, and Evan could feel the contentment settle into him as Josh's shoulders relaxed. "Good," he finally murmured.

They stayed like that for a good minute or two, just cradling each other. A smile crept over Evan's lips, and he finally turned his head to gaze up at Josh. "I wanna give this a real shot. I want a label."

"You want to be boyfriends?" Josh looked surprised, and he wasn't quick enough to hide the pleased and hopeful look in his eyes.

That look made Evan want to do anything for him. "Yeah. Yeah, I do."

"Deal." Josh squeezed him tightly. "And no take-backsies."

The sudden caveat, uttered as seriously as if it were a relationship dealbreaker instead of a playground game, made Evan laugh until he couldn't breathe.

"And this is why I love you," he finally said.

"Really?" Josh grinned. "I thought it was the great sex."

Oh, the heat that prickled through him at the simple

word was impossible to contain. Evan wondered if this honeymoon phase would ever fade—he sure hoped not. It felt like his first boyfriend all over again, like they were exploring all the possibilities together with fresh eyes and open hearts.

"You make me feel new again."

"Like a virgin?" Josh quipped.

"Touched for the very first time."

Josh smirked and ran his hands up Evan's back, under his shirt. "I'll touch you for the very first time. We've got time, right?"

"An hour, at least." Evan squirmed and laughed as Josh found his nipples. "Oh, fuck. You're going for the kill."

"There's no time to waste. An hour could mean two orgasms, if we plan this right." Josh pulled both nipples until Evan squirmed and gasped and stood up.

"Fuck!" Evan tried to bat away Josh's hands, but he was determined. "They ain't a damn collar."

"Now you're picking up my slang." Josh winked. "But no. If I wanted a collar on you, I'd find one."

Evan smirked. "You should be so lucky." Then a groan escaped. It was hard to be sassy and defiant when Josh had him by the sensitive nubs, and was slowly rubbing his thumbs around and across them.

"Bedroom," Josh ordered, and Evan was happy to listen.

They nearly tumbled onto the bed together, stripping off their clothes as fast as they could manage. Their arms kept getting tangled in the process, and Evan couldn't stop laughing.

Sex was silly and fun and *joyful* with Josh. He'd never realized it could be, before him.

"God, I love you," he whispered, half to himself, after

they'd finally gotten all those stupid clothes out of the way. "Even if you're always making fun of me."

Josh smiled. "I love you, even if you're the clumsiest guy I've known. And a terrible horseback rider, too. I'll work on that."

"See? Now you're making fun of me again." Evan flopped on his back and covered his face. "I don't know why I put up with you." The hot, wet mouth that closed around the head of his half-excited cock startled him into a gasp as Josh answered that question silently. "Fuck!"

When he peeked through his fingers, Josh was bobbing his head down to the bottom of his shaft, taking the whole thing into his mouth in one gulp.

"Oh my *God*. Fuck. Fine." It was so damn sensitive, and Evan squirmed so badly, that Josh had to press a hand on his stomach to hold him down. "You made your point."

Josh's answer sounded a lot like, "Mmngh." He didn't relent—just ran his tongue around the head as Evan's cock grew hard almost painfully fast.

Sensation raced from the tip of Evan's cock through his groin, lighting a fire deep inside that danced along his skin. His cheeks burned, and his breathing quickened. Every slick slide of Josh's lips along his shaft, and every curl of his tongue around the head, made Evan just about lose his damn mind.

He couldn't hold out for long, and he knew it. He tried to drag out the minutes of ecstasy, but before long, he squeezed Josh's shoulders. "Fuck. I'm nearly there."

"Good," Josh whispered across his sensitive cock head, one hand curled tightly around the shaft. "I want to taste you."

And just like that, he wrung another orgasm out of Evan

with his hand and mouth, leaving Evan trembling and grinning at nothing at all.

"Good?" Josh asked as he licked his lips, kissing his way up Evan's body to rest his head on his shoulder.

"Amazing," Evan corrected him. "Even if you're a smart-ass, you're a smart-ass who can suck cock with the best of them."

Josh snickered. "That needs to be my tag line. Or warning label."

"Both." Evan patted Josh's hip. "Scoot up. Fuck my mouth."

Josh's breath caught in his throat, and he just about kneed Evan in the stomach as he scrambled up the bed. "You sure?" he asked as he knelt over Evan's chest. His expression was full of the kind of eager anticipation that made Evan hot, even if he'd just finished.

Evan grinned up at him. "Never been surer."

He closed his eyes and wrapped his lips around Josh's cock, trying not to grin. God, sex with Josh always felt good. When he was with Josh, Evan felt both desired and respected —a combination that was often hard to find.

When Josh finally came, Evan didn't let him pull away. Swallowing might have nothing to do with love, but he happened to fucking love doing it. And the reaction from Josh was well worth it.

"Wow," was all Josh could manage. He leaned on the headboard, propping himself up weakly. "I... wow."

Evan grinned. "Speechless? That's rare."

"Hey," Josh snorted. He finally flopped onto the bed and tried to tickle Evan, but he was sluggish and Evan easily squirmed away. "If that's what having you *completely and utterly in love* gets me..."

"Oh, my God. You're gonna hold that over me forever." Evan sighed at him.

Josh smirked. "Yeah, I am. Not every day you overhear a confession of deep and passionate love."

"You know the context!" Evan protested. He pulled one of Josh's pillows over his face again.

"Yeah, I do." Josh didn't stop laughing. "You're adorable when you're shy, you know."

Evan muttered, "Fuck off."

"Why does talking about love make you shy?"

Evan took a few moments to realize that Josh wasn't teasing anymore. It was a genuine question, and he didn't mind answering those kinds of questions. Not from Josh, anyway. "Because…" He pulled the pillow away and settled on it, wrapping his arm around Josh's shoulder to stay close. "I'm not sure."

"I don't always say what I mean either." Josh was watching him steadily now. "But I do know what I feel. And I love you. Maybe not in the *marry me and have my babies* way yet, we'll see. But there's something here I want to explore."

Evan's breath rushed out, and the tension he hadn't even known he was holding did, too. "Yes. Me, too."

"So let's see where this goes." Josh smiled. "I mean, your family sure as hell knows already. My brothers…"

Evan laughed. "They guessed." They hadn't been wrong, but it was gonna piss off Josh a little bit to admit it. Poor guy.

Josh rubbed Evan's shoulder, his fingers trailing along the skin in small circles. "And if things change, well, we'll figure it out then."

"Like if I realize this is a rebound? I don't think so," Evan told him, sticking his chin out defiantly. "You're not getting away from me that easily."

Josh's smile flickered, but it stayed. "Oh?"

"You can't make out that this is all lust." Evan shook his head. "Or we would've fucked and gone our different ways."

"Yeah," Josh admitted, laughing quietly. "I've done that enough times. I didn't think this would be any different. That *you'd* be any different."

Evan nodded before he'd even finished speaking. He sure as hell hadn't expected anything more than a new friend and maybe some hot sex. Somehow, he'd scored a boyfriend. "Exactly. And then…"

"Life laughed at us?" Josh suggested, his lips quirking.

"It did."

Silence fell for a few moments as they held each other, but there was nothing uncomfortable about it—just an easy acceptance of this new status quo.

"Okay, we'd better get dressed and ready for Gina to come back. If we're still in bed when she comes back, I bet she'd tease you for way longer than I will," Josh told Evan with a grin.

He wasn't wrong. Evan scrambled for his clothes as Josh laughed. He tossed Josh's shirt at him, which ignited a match of Josh trying to play keep-away with his jeans.

How the hell had he wound up with this guy as a boyfriend? And why did his face hurt from smiling?

Gina was right: at long last, Evan was happy.

CHAPTER
Twenty~Three

JOSH

"WHY'D YOU TELL MY FUCKING PARENTS I BLEW OFF WORK today?"

Adam's attitude was so expected that Josh just smiled as Adam thumped and stomped his way into reception.

Ryanna raised her eyebrows and folded her arms, looking back and forth between Adam and Josh. Between everyone who'd come stomping in today demanding answers, she was getting a hell of a show.

"Rather than telling them I fired you a few weeks ago?" Josh asked, keeping his voice level. "And telling them what you and a certain Mr. Smith have been getting up to?"

Adam went pale. He clearly tried to hide it by huffing and grunting, "Dunno what you mean," but the shock was unmistakable.

God, Josh almost felt bad for him. He was a dumb kid who'd gotten in over his head.

"Don't play dumb. I respect you more than that. Respect yourself more than that, too," Josh advised him coolly. "This is all gonna come out in court otherwise, and your parents will be a lot more pissed than they are now. Come into my office and talk for a minute." He jerked his head toward the open office door, then turned and walked inside.

Adam hesitated but followed, closing the door after himself. He slouched his way into the chair, looking like a deer in the headlights.

Josh knew the feeling. He sat behind the desk and looked around at the paperwork strewn across it: insurance company documents, copies of Mona's last year of veterinary reports, and all. He let Adam follow his gaze and look at them for a minute, too. He had a feeling Adam hadn't really thought through his revenge plan.

"I didn't do anything," Adam muttered, but it was the statement a rebellious teen would make.

"Are you willing to testify to that in court? Keeping in mind that any evidence to the contrary—CCTV, testimonials, Mr. Smith breaking down and confessing the plan—will mean some pretty serious charges against you?"

Adam went pale again and said nothing.

Josh let the silence drag on for a good minute before he leaned in. "Being fired sucks. I get it. But you ain't gonna make things better by doing this."

"You're just trying to get me to confess."

"I don't need you to," Josh said, chuckling. "The insurance company is already on the case. An old injury—whiplash, being dropped on his head as a kid, I don't know what— won't show up the same. If the doctors haven't already gotten wind of it, they will. Social media smear campaigns won't work, either. But if you don't wanna talk about why you did it, answer me this: why haven't you told your parents you got fired?"

Adam stared down at the desk, his arms tightly folded. At

last, a good ten seconds later, he looked up. "How'd you know I didn't?"

"I went to your house and they got scared shitless something had happened to you at work. Especially your mom. She burst into tears."

That, at least, seemed to puncture Adam's inflated sense of victimization with a little well-placed guilt. "Shit," he muttered.

"Yeah. So I said no, you weren't in, and I was already in town, so I thought I'd drop by and make sure everything's fine. And then I assume you got home and they chewed you out."

Adam's gaze was back on his desk. Josh knew how it felt —like being a toddler, or maybe a surly first-grader hauled into the principal's office, sitting in the little chair opposite the desk from the guy you most wanted to tell to go fuck himself.

He'd felt it enough from his dad. He didn't want to be that kind of dad himself—nor boss, nor friend, nor lover.

He could be better than that.

Josh dug deep, scrambling to figure out what to say—how to handle this right. He only had one shot. God, it had only been a decade ago he'd been Adam's age, frustrated and lashing out at everything around him, with nobody to talk to about everything.

He could handle it in court, but that was a shitty way of winning. He didn't want to destroy some kid's life just because he'd been dumb, even if that kid had almost destroyed *his* life. That wouldn't make him the better person here.

"Why are you afraid of your parents finding out?" he asked again.

Finally, a chink in Adam's armor. He flinched, then shifted restlessly a few times. When it became clear Josh was waiting for an answer, he sighed. "They'd kick my ass six ways from Sunday. Hell, they did today and they don't even know..."

Josh nodded slightly. "Physically, or...?"

"No," Adam was quick to answer, straightening up. "Hell, naw. Just the way any parent would, you know?"

"You can't put off the inevitable forever. If they found out what you've started," Josh waved at this paperwork, "you'd be in serious shit."

"I wasn't thinking." Adam's voice cracked, and he slumped forward. "I'm supposed to be the good guy, the perfect kid. My brother, he wound up in jail. But I'm the one who's keeping his nose clean and doing everything right. They'll bake him a fucking cake for not breaking probation, but I get good grades and I just get a *could be better*, right? And if I can't keep a job, I gotta enlist. Those are my options. Ain't nobody else hiring around here. Not when you can go to stupid fuckin' college and get two degrees and still get stuck as some shitty job as a Starbucks barista for the rest of your life."

Josh nodded along. "So why even bother? If they don't seem to care what you do, and nothing you do is good enough?"

Adam sucked his breath in slowly, as if hearing those words for real. "Yeah. It sounds stupid when you put it that way..."

"It's not stupid," Josh said quietly. "Not one bit. You know anything about how I got to own this place?"

"They say your dad died a few years back?" Adam offered

cautiously. He was finally looking up, though not quite meeting his gaze. It was a start.

"Yep. I all but ran away to college before that. Dad hated that I was gay, hated that I was a lazy asshole, hated everything I did. Never got to make it up to him." He could see the stoniness on Adam's face, and he smiled slightly. "I'm not making this a *make up with them before it's too late* thing, man, I promise." He chuckled. "Not sure Dad and I could have ever made up, to be honest. Not after some of the stuff he said, and some of the stuff I did."

He licked his lips and glanced down at the desk, then back up at Adam. *He doesn't need to know all those details.*

"But I know what it's like to be afraid of your parents. And you've got one more than I did, which has gotta be even worse."

"If it's not one yelling at me to get better grades, it's the other saying I ain't getting a free ride."

Josh leaned back and folded his arms. "And when they find out you got fired, it's straight to the recruitment office."

"Yep. They won't be crying," Adam muttered.

Military might not be bad to straighten this kid out, but it could also completely shatter him. He'd seen that, too. And without any real family support, it could just be a way of washing their hands of him. Kinda like Dad had washed his hands of Josh by letting him go off to school.

Nobody should get treated like that. Josh knew it was a stupid idea, but he couldn't stop himself. "Unless they don't find out."

Adam looked up and furrowed his brows. "Huh?"

"I can't afford to pay someone to not turn up."

Adam had the grace to look ashamed of that, at least. He

looked down and nodded. "I shouldn't have skipped so much work."

"But I can't afford for work not to get done. It's a fine line. And when all this shit happens…" Josh pointed at the papers again, drawing Adam's gaze. "That bullshit? It costs me money. And then I can't pay my staff who *do* turn up."

Adam folded his arms tightly, his cheeks scarlet red.

Josh backed off. Adam clearly regretted it, even if he wasn't going to outright apologize. He had too much pride for that. Josh knew what it was like to be caught up in your own fear about what would happen if you had to apologize, and admit you were in the wrong.

Whether or not Adam could bring himself to do the right thing in the end, he seemed to be getting through, and berating him wouldn't help a damn thing.

"So, I hired a kid. Kev. He needed a place to live and a job. He's living in cabin twelve. He's aware that he'll have to share the place with anyone else who needs the same."

Adam's expression of hope, quickly hidden, just about broke Josh's heart. He clearly wanted this badly, but he didn't think he deserved it.

Maybe he didn't. But maybe he did. Whatever he said about his parents just being normal parents, the kid had hidden something as ordinary as getting fired from his first job from them for weeks.

Josh didn't need to know his life story or the depths of his pain to know he needed help.

"*If* I invite you back, I gotta know that I can trust you. No more of this not showing up on sunny days bullshit. You know you can do better than that. So do your parents, even if they've got a fucked-up way of showing it."

Adam still stared down.

"And you gotta learn to ask for help, not lash out. You don't deserve a second chance—not because of who you are, but because of what you've done to me. But I'm giving it to you anyway. Do *not* fuck me over, or I'm gonna see what I can do legally, and I'll tell your parents everything."

"You're… giving me a job?" Adam sounded bewildered.

"And a place to live. Can't pay you much since room and board is included, but it's your own roof—shared with a roommate, until and unless Kev leaves, or maybe someone else. You keep your nose clean. No drinking, no drugs, no partying. I pay you, I help you figure out what you like doing around here and you do more of it. Sometimes you do the shitty work because you fucking earned that when you started all this bullshit. Speaking of which, you call Mr. Smith right now and tell him the game's up."

Despite the harsh words, Adam was sitting up straighter. Josh's instinct that he could rise to the reasonable demands seemed to be correct. "Are you serious?"

"Dead serious. I'll draw up a contract right now. And I won't tell your parents about these couple weeks you had *off work*," Josh added. "Joining the military ain't always a bad thing. But if you join—if you do any kind of work, I don't care what it is, but especially something that will risk your life—it should be on your own terms. Not because someone wants to dump you like an unwanted sack of potatoes."

Shit. That was what Adam and Kev had in common, and it took saying it out loud for Josh to realize that it was his weak spot. He couldn't say no to someone who felt like they didn't matter, and who needed a chance to *be* someone.

Adam flinched—harder than he had even the first time. His arms were half-wrapped around himself.

Josh had never seen him this vulnerable, and it was half-terrifying. He didn't want to break down his confidence, but he wanted to break through his ego. How the fuck did parents do this?

His dad suddenly seemed a lot larger in his mind. Yeah, he'd made shitty choices long before Josh had developed an attitude, but those final rifts between them? They suddenly seemed a lot more understandable.

"Okay." Adam's voice was small. He cleared his throat and sat up straighter, his next words gruff. "Yeah. I can do that."

Josh nodded once and reached a hand out. "Word of honor," he warned Adam. "You stabbed me in the back once. I don't give third chances, and I won't go easy on you. Only promise me if you're gonna live up to it."

"Yeah." Adam took his hand with a strong grip. "Yeah, I can do that." When he let go, he took his phone out. "I guess I'll... how do I...?"

"Tell Mr. Smith I found out what's going on. You guys are Facebook friends," Josh told him, his lips quirking into a smile. "Did you know that? The rest was easy to guess."

"Ah, shit," Adam mumbled.

Josh tried not to laugh. They weren't exactly criminal masterminds. He had no idea how they'd known each other or why they'd both been dumb enough to think it would work, but as satisfying as it would be to see an asshole like Mr. Smith get torn apart in court, it would come at a heavy price to Adam—and to Josh himself.

No. No more rifts—not when he didn't need them. He'd stretch out a hand, and if it got bitten... well, at least he'd tried.

"Kev around?" He poked his head out the office door.

"He's checking the fence line around the back field."

"When he gets back, tell him he's got a roommate. I want

them to meet." Josh glanced back at Adam. "And we've got a new employee. Old new employee. Adam—you're back."

Ryanna looked startled, but she hid her surprise with a small smile. "Hello again. Uhhh. Welcome back?"

Adam raised a hand in a small wave. "Hey. Mind if I go outside and make a quick phone call?"

Josh gestured with a smile. "Go right ahead." In the meantime, Ryanna was giving him a look that meant he had a lot of explaining to do.

CHAPTER
Twenty~Four

EVAN

"So I'm pretty sure this guy's batshit crazy, but in the opposite way as Monty. I see why you love him. Utterly and completely." Gina gave Evan a wicked grin as she pointed her fork at Josh.

Josh snickered. "I'll take that as a compliment."

"Oh yeah. Monty wouldn't hire the asshole who tried to get him sued. He'd drag him to the square for a flogging. Though, I dunno… I haven't seen any stocks around here… maybe you've got them hidden. Like, in your bedroom?" Gina squinted out the farmhouse window.

Evan slumped lower in his chair. "Traffic's gonna be bad. You don't wanna hang around too much longer."

"Is my darling baby brother trying to get rid of me?" Gina tsked and shook her head. "You should know that doesn't work. Breakfast was great, though!" She finished her orange juice and checked her watch.

"Got time for more embarrassing family stories?" Josh sounded hopeful, damn him.

"No, she doesn't," Evan said, as pointedly as he could.

Gina laughed. "Unfortunately, I don't. I gotta get back for work tomorrow."

"Shit, that's a hard drive." Josh frowned. "You gonna be okay?"

"Honey, I've driven more miles than you've probably dreamed of." Gina flashed him a grin. In her last job, in sales, she'd been all over the country. Evan might have guessed she'd drive down just to check on him—if not because of Mom's orders. "I can do twice that and clean up just fine for a sales meeting in the morning."

Josh glanced between them and shook his head.

"What?" Evan asked.

"You guys make me feel like a slacker, that's all." Josh laughed self-consciously.

"The guy who runs a ranch?" Evan raised his eyebrow. "Bullshit."

"I'm just a ranch kid who hated work. Now it's a fake ranch." Josh laughed, but this time more in amusement at himself.

"Nope," Gina declared. "You've got a four-and-a-half rating on TripAdvisor. About the same on three other sites."

Josh smiled. "Huh. You did your homework." He glanced at Evan. "The similarities are impressive."

"Duh. Cut from the same cloth. Only Evan went the quiet nerdy way and I went the brash way." Gina winked. "Most people mistake the quietness for not having anything to say."

"Not me," Josh murmured. "I might be a loudmouth myself, but I respect the hell out of that."

Evan blushed as they both looked at him. "Are we done psychoanalyzing me?"

"For now. I gotta hit the road. But you're both coming

back for Thanksgiving, right?" The look Gina shot them both made it clear it wasn't optional.

Josh saluted. "Yes, ma'am. If there's a turkey and stuffing…"

Evan knew it was coming, but it didn't stop Gina from saying it. "That's what Evan's been missing lately. Some good stuffing."

"Happy to help him get his life back on track."

"I thought you might be."

"Go away," Evan moaned, but he couldn't help laughing, too. "Thank you for coming to check on me, but I'm just fine. Tell Mom not to worry."

"I will. I'll tell her how adorable you two are, and then you'll have to come for Thanksgiving," Gina warned Josh.

"Have to come get delicious food and listen to more of this sibling banter?" Josh smirked. "I think I can manage that."

"Great." As she stood, Josh moved to shake hands, and she snorted and pulled him in for a hug instead.

"You're not escaping this so easily."

Josh's lips quirked into a smile. "Funny. I heard that not long ago, too. The two of you really are peas in a pod."

More than Evan had remembered, Josh was right. God, it was nice to talk to them again—to hang out without the fear of what Monty would say about her later, or what she might say to Monty's face, or how he could do damage control.

He didn't have to *manage* people or situations anymore. He never had needed to, except to hold together a failing relationship. He could just *be*, and be himself, and the people around him liked him for it.

Josh waved goodbye, and Evan walked Gina down to her car, carrying her bag for her. He was getting to know the place—every cabin he passed felt familiar, and he didn't spot any employees he hadn't already met. He exchanged smiles and nods with the guests he passed.

In a couple of weeks, this place had gotten to feel more like home than his old Manhattan penthouse ever had.

"I'm sorry about the stuff he sent home." Evan grimaced. "I didn't know he was serious about wanting a forwarding address."

"Fuck that shit," Gina muttered. "If I'd known, I would've picked it up myself, so I could kick him in the balls so hard his grandkids feel it. If they're ever unlucky enough to exist."

Evan smiled and put his arm around Gina's shoulders. "It's been great to see you again, if only for like... thirty seconds."

Gina laughed. "Yeah. Just long enough to make sure you're *you* again. And you are, thank God."

"Yeah," Evan agreed, and they stopped by the driver's side door to hug tightly.

"Don't let him sweep you totally off your feet. We still want you to come home," Gina told him.

Evan winked and echoed Josh. "Aye aye, ma'am."

"If it's a rebound, I don't give a shit. You're happy. He's happy. The world goes on turning." Gina pulled back and looked him in the eye. "And you're being true to yourself again. Don't let that go."

"I won't," Evan promised in a murmur. Josh wouldn't let him, and that fact made him smile. Josh was the man he'd been waiting his whole life to meet, and he'd never known.

After waving Gina off, Evan put his hands in his pockets and strolled back up the dusty Main Street of the ranch, taking his time to admire it like he'd never seen it before.

Rustic touches were everywhere: the wheel balanced

against the side of the barn, the hay bales stacked between cabins, and the cowboy boots that sat on every porch. But the vaguely cheesy Wild West theme did nothing to take away from the rural atmosphere that was already here, and Evan had a feeling *that* was what kept people coming back for more.

As he gazed across the fields toward the blue-hazed mountains rising in the distance, Evan felt it once more: peace.

This was easy in a way he'd never known. His heart and soul were at peace with his decision to stay here, and what's more, he was excited about it.

For years, even if the bills had been covered, he'd just coasted by. Never really got excited about anything. Never had a reason to feel angry, or sad, or anything besides *frustrated but patient for Monty's sake.*

Sure, Josh wasn't perfect. But nobody was. Neither was Evan. They'd both admitted as much already, and they weren't going to let each other get away with being a dick. Nor would they jump down each other's throat for it. He didn't have to be afraid of repercussions anymore for being… well, human.

Sudden movement and noise made him nearly jump out of his skin.

Kev and Adam burst out of the door, chatting loudly about some car thing—an imaginary drag race, it sounded like.

"—out of your mind? The torque is *way* higher."

"Nuh uh," Kev fiercely defended himself. "That piece of shit would lose every time."

They both stopped dead at the sight of Evan, who just laughed and waved. "I don't know the faintest thing about what you mean, but if you ain't drag-racing Josh's tractors, I don't care."

Kev laughed, and the sound made Evan smile. God, if it weren't for Kev, he might not have realized that the telltale moments of jealousy added up to something more.

How fucking weird and great life was.

"I meant to ask," Kev said as they approached. "You're from New York?"

"Vermont originally, but yeah, I lived there for years."

Kev's eyes lit up in the way that only a small-town kid's could. "What's it like there?"

Evan smiled and leaned on the porch railing as Kev crouched on the step, pulling his dusty boots on. "It's not for me. But for some people, it's just right. Thinking of moving there?"

"I got a buddy who's a mechanic out there." Kev jerked his thumb at Adam. "This guy thinks he's full of shit. I dared him to prove him wrong."

"A long way to go for just a drag race," Evan pointed out. He knew damn well it wasn't just about that, though. Were these guys thinking of leaving?

"Well... I promised to stay here until Christmas, at least." Kev frowned. "But in the spring, maybe we can go."

"The spring's a long way off."

"Gives me time to save up."

"If you want to move there, then do it," Evan told him, glancing between them. "That goes for either of you. It'll be wilder and more expensive and better than you imagined. Or maybe worse. Either way, you'll never know if you don't do it."

Kev straightened up again and tugged his hat down over his eyes. "Maybe I will."

Adam, who had barely moved in before finding Evan for an awkward sort-of-apology, and who had been on his best behavior in the two days since, awkwardly nodded. "Maybe I will, too. We don't know."

Evan smiled. "No need to decide yet. I better let you get to work. We'll talk more about New York over the winter."

"Awesome. Thanks." Kev shot him a grin and took off for the barn, with Adam hot on his heels.

Evan made his way back up to the house, casting one more look and smile around at the place. Time to call his lawyer friend and see if they were in the clear. Josh would grumble about taking favors from people, but Evan could tell he was grateful.

Like it or not, Josh was stuck with him now. If he had one string left from his old life to pull for Josh's sake, he'd do it.

He dialed Taylor as he walked. "Hey, it's Evan. Just calling about the Smith case."

"Oh, I meant to send you an email."

"Hey, it's fine. Pro bono stuff comes last," Evan said. "I really appreciate your time."

"No problem. Anything for an old buddy. As long as you don't tell Monty I did this for you."

Evan chuckled. He more than understood the intricate political machinations at work. "Of course."

"I called the other guy, had a little chat. Told him all the stuff you've found out. Everything's going to go away quietly. The insurance company might go after Smith for wasting their damn time, but the kid's probably free and clear. If I hear anything more, I'll give you a shout."

"Good. That's awesome news." Evan made his way up the farmhouse steps. "Thanks a million."

"Anytime. I hope this Josh guy's worth it for you. You were never gonna have a good life with Monty."

Of course he'd guessed at the real reason Evan was willing to do all this for him. But it somehow hadn't occurred to Evan that anyone from Monty's life might have noticed what an asshole his ex-fiancé was.

"Oh, yeah. He is."

"Good. I'm glad for you. Say hi when you're in town again."

Evan never planned to be in town again, but he chuckled. "I will. You too, if you're ever in Knoxville."

"You never know. I hear it's got a great dude ranch. I got buddies with bachelor parties. If I ever need to piss off Monty to get my way on something…"

Evan laughed. "Feel free to come on down. Talk to you later, Taylor."

He hung up and stepped inside Josh's house—*his* house now, too.

"All good?" Josh was shrugging on the plaid shirt that meant he was about to leave for work.

And Evan had a full day of work ahead of him, pulling together a whole new brand for the ranch.

He smiled and slid his arms around Josh's waist, letting the door close behind him as he leaned in for a kiss. "Really good. I just called Taylor. The whole fucking mess is going away now. Insurance might come after Smith for the fraud, but you should be clear."

Josh let out a long sigh of relief and rubbed Evan's back. "That calls for a celebration, I think. Beer in the hot tub tonight?"

"I'll RSVP yes to that any day." Evan kissed Josh. "Come

back at lunchtime and I'll show you my new branding concept."

"I can't wait to see."

"Love you, baby."

Josh beamed at him—the kind of grin that made him look even more impossibly gorgeous than he had the first moment Evan had seen him. "Love you, too." He kissed Evan once more and bounded out the front door. "Hold that thought 'til tonight."

"Oh, I will." Evan leaned on the porch railing to wave goodbye to Josh, more playfully than anything else. They saw each other several times a day now—not that either of them could have resisted being away from each other for long.

Ah, that honeymoon phase. Evan planned to enjoy every minute of it. As he turned his face to the sun, he decided to grab his laptop and work out on the porch. Might as well soak up this autumn sunshine while it lasted.

Yeah. It was gonna be a long day, but a good one. Evan could feel it in his bones.

Twenty~Five

JOSH

"I'm gonna figure out a way to pay you properly. I don't like the idea of having a bunch of guys working, and me not paying them well."

"Sounds like work talk." Evan smiled at Josh and wagged his finger at him. "This is hot tub time."

Josh laughed. "Are we implementing a new rule? No work talk in the hot tub?" Some of his best work ideas had come from hot tub time, but it might not be a bad idea. The last thing he wanted was for Evan to get sick and tired of the business.

"I've got the new campaign off the ground. We're seeing some clicks already," Evan told Josh. The way he scooted through the water to sit on his lap, knowing full well they were both naked, was very distracting.

"It'll take time. I've got patience," Josh told him. "Sometimes."

Evan grinned wolfishly. "I know you do, sometimes." He looped his arms around Josh's neck after plucking the beer out of his hand. "Sometimes I don't."

"Getting down to business—er, non-business—already?" Josh winked. "I can't believe branding makes you that hot under the collar."

Evan laughed. "Me neither. There's something about a website redesign that makes me hard."

Though Josh laughed, even the idea of Evan getting hard was enough to get *him* hard—and being on his lap, Evan noticed.

"We'd better get out of the tub," Josh chuckled, kissing Evan slowly.

Evan ground against him slowly, the hot water sloshing between their bodies as he found a comfortable angle to do so. When his hand closed around both of their shafts, Josh gasped and moaned.

"Don't want our precum clogging the filters?" Evan teased.

Josh laughed breathlessly. "Yeah."

Evan grinned. "I suppose you've got a point." He pulled back and stood up, then climbed out of the hot tub—which was an incredible view, especially when he was hard.

"Jesus. I want a photo of that."

Evan laughed, but Josh shook his head. "For real. Your boner standing up against the early twilight stars…"

"You're making it sound like art now."

Josh grinned. If it weren't a weird idea, he'd ask Falcon how he felt about painting boners. "My favorite kind of art. Besides yours."

"Pffft. Mine's all business," Evan shook his head.

After one glance at Evan's portfolio, Josh anticipated an uptick in business with him on the case. When that happened, he wouldn't let Evan be modest for long. "Mmm," he answered vaguely and winked, then smacked that sexy ass. "Off to my room with you."

"While dripping wet?" Evan managed to make even the way he wrapped himself in a towel look sensual, the folds of the towel draping along the curves of his body—and the distinctive tent in the front.

"Fuck, that's hot," Josh whispered.

"You want it in you, or bobbing in the air under you?" Evan winked when Josh glanced up quickly.

Josh swallowed hard. "Either sounds… um, epic."

"I'll let you top first," Evan offered with a cheeky smile.

Josh laughed. There was no orgasm quite like the kind that rushed through him when a cock was inside him. He didn't blame Evan for wanting the first turn on the bottom. "How gracious."

"I know. I'm willing to make that sacrifice," Evan teased. "That's how much I love you." He wiggled his ass and darted inside, flashing a grin over his shoulder.

Josh smirked and followed, but he wasn't in a hurry to chase him. At last, it wasn't just talk—he really felt like he had all the time in the world with Evan.

Once he'd turned off the hot tub and gathered their empty beer bottles, Josh shut the patio door with a soft click and listened for footsteps. None, which meant he must be already waiting in the bedroom. Good. Let him feel the anticipation. It would make what was coming even better.

When he walked into the room, Josh's breath caught in his throat. Evan was standing in front of the full-length mirror, the towel cast aside, running his hands up to his throat and through his hair. As Josh watched, he traced his hands along his chest, playing with his nipples for a few moments, and then down to his thighs. His fingertips grazed his cock, which stood hard and flushed in the air.

"That's the prettiest thing I've seen in my life," Josh murmured. He sidled into the room and shut the door behind him, letting his steps stay slow and patient.

Seeing Evan touch himself made something under Josh's skin want to take over. He wanted to make Evan feel as blissful as he found him beautiful, but he reminded himself that that was coming soon.

Evan's fingertips trailed along his collarbone and down his arm as he turned to look at himself sideways in the mirror, wiggling his ass back and forth again. Josh closed one hand around his throbbing cock to support himself as he approached, making eye contact with Evan in the mirror.

Whatever Evan saw in his eyes, he liked it. He gasped and pressed backward into Josh, his body rippling in a fluid line from the back of his neck to his torso as they made contact. And God, the warm, damp skin against skin was the closest to heaven Josh had ever been.

He held Evan close for a few moments, cradling his body with an arm around his waist. His other hand ran up Evan's stomach to his chest to play with his nipple. The more delicately he touched it, the more Evan gasped and squirmed in his arms, which was rewarding when that sexy little ass was pressing up against his hard shaft.

"You better fuck me soon," Evan warned.

"Or what?" Josh smirked and kissed his shoulder. "I think I've got the upper hand here."

In one quick move, Evan pulled away just enough to slip his hand behind himself—and how was he that flexible? Had Josh known he was that flexible? He definitely would have remembered. Evan gripped his shaft and pulled it between his thighs, squeezing tightly around Josh's cock as he rocked back against him again.

Damn it, that felt good. Josh moaned softly, but he pinched Evan's nipple. "If you're not careful, I might just slip in."

Evan snickered. "I half-considered lubing up before you came in."

"That would have been an amazing sight to walk in on." Josh could picture it already. "I dare you to do that sometime."

"Double doggy dare?" Evan bent at the waist for a moment and rocked back into Josh before he straightened up, looking for all the world like a graceful dancer. Josh would have to ask if he knew any dance sometime. Not now, though. He wasn't sure he could get the words out.

The shifting tight pressure around his shaft made Josh gasp, his nails digging into Evan's hips. "Oh, yeah. Any way you like, baby."

"Finger me," Evan whispered. "And then you can fuck my tight little ass. I need you tonight."

Josh's grin almost hurt his cheeks. He wanted to be there for Evan any which way he needed him, but this was a particularly rewarding one. He stumbled for the lube, and by the time he'd made it back, Evan had stepped over to stand next to the bed.

Evan caught his eye and then bent over, bracing his forearms on the edge of the bed and looking sideways at the mirror again. Josh had never been so glad for the decision to install one.

Josh ran his nails gently down Evan's back as he slid two slick fingers around his pulsating hole. Every time Evan clenched or pushed back, Josh pulled his fingers away.

Teasing the sensitive nerve endings there was his favorite foreplay. He didn't want to satisfy Evan too easily.

On the other hand, Evan was pushing back into him with needy moans that Josh couldn't ignore any longer. "Please," Evan panted. He twisted to gaze over his shoulder, meeting Josh's eyes with a pleading expression.

Josh couldn't resist those eyes. As gently as he could, he slid one finger past tight rings of muscle, taking it slowly despite Evan pushing back into him for more.

"I can handle a hell of a lot more," Evan muttered.

"I know you can, darling. But not tonight." Josh rubbed between his shoulder blades. "Tonight, I want to spoil you."

"Spoil me with your cock? Hard and fast?"

"We'll get there," Josh promised with a laugh. He slid a second finger in, waiting until Evan rocked his hips back before he started rubbing in slow, gentle circles around his prostate.

Evan gasped and pushed back, starting to squirm under him again. "Oh, yeah. Baby, don't make me come too quick."

"It's tempting," Josh admitted, grinning as he pressed down on Evan's lower back to keep him in place so he didn't hurt himself. "But not today." He slicked his fingers, his heart racing as he ran them down his shaft, then pushed against Evan's entrance.

"Yes," Evan panted. "Jesus, before I lose my damn mind waiting!"

Tightness closed in around Josh as he pushed inside. "Oh, God. You feel so good, Evan," he murmured. "You're perfect."

Evan giggled under his breath. "I dunno about that, but you'll find that out sooner or later."

"I can't wait," Josh told him with a grin, and he meant it. Every rough, unfinished edge on Evan was another little hidden gem. As far as Josh was concerned, any piece of Evan's spirit he got to see was a good piece.

He set his hips into a slow, steady motion, pressing Evan into the side of the bed until Evan's cock was trapped between his stomach and the comforter. With every thrust, Evan's whimpers echoed from the walls of his bedroom—the most stunning sound Josh had ever heard.

Josh wanted to wrap his arms around Evan and hold him tight forever. However the hell Evan would let him be there for him, that was what Josh would do. If he could put a ring on it, then hell yeah, that was what he'd do. Evan was intoxicating in a way he'd never known, and he would never be able to give up now.

"I love you," Josh whispered, wrapping his hands around Evan's hips.

Evan grinned back over his shoulder. "If you love me, fuck me like you mean it."

Josh pushed his hips forward harder, thrusting deeper and faster until Evan's cocky grin turned into gasps of pleasure.

They were in a world of their own now, losing themselves in the world they'd found. Before long, Josh pulled out of Evan, rolling him over and helping him scoot up the bed. Sinking back between his legs and inside was perfection all over again. It meant they lost sight of the mirror, but they could look in each other's eyes.

As he pushed himself deep inside Evan, he saw every expression of arousal and pleasure flickering across his boyfriend's face.

"I'm so lucky to have you," Josh whispered.

Evan's smile deepened until those adorable dimples appeared. "I'm lucky, too, you know."

Josh wasn't going to argue the point while he was sweaty and out of breath and so on-edge he was about to burst. He wanted so badly to give in to the pleasure that threatened to drag him under, but he also wanted to make it last for Evan.

Not that Evan was going to be much longer. He squirmed until he could get a hand between their bodies, and then he jerked himself off fast and hard.

Josh matched the pace of his hand, pounding into Evan and staying as quiet as he could so he could hear every whimper and moan from those beautiful lips.

Finally, as he ran one hand over Evan's chest to play with his nipples, Evan gasped and spilled over the edge, and Josh could let go, too.

Orgasm brought blissful relief, and the kind of warm, fuzzy feelings he'd never expected to consume him—let alone right after sex. As soon as Josh was soft enough to slide out of Evan, he cuddled him fiercely.

Evan laughed breathlessly as he rubbed Josh's shoulder and the back of his neck. "I love you too, hon."

Had Josh said it? Or had he just shown it with his body language? He had no idea anymore. He grinned as he flopped onto his side and scooped Evan up in a bear hug. "Mine."

"Yeah," Evan whispered, pressing his chest into Josh's chest. "Yours."

That was all Josh needed to hear. He closed his eyes and breathed in the scent of his lover as they cooled off together.

If this was love, he hadn't been missing out—he'd just been waiting for the right timing. For the right guy to fall into his lap. Or throw up on his shoes. Same difference, right?

When Evan prompted Josh to explain his chuckles, he just

shook his head. There was plenty of time to tease him later. "I'm just glad you're in it with me."

"For the long haul," Evan murmured, pressing his nose into Josh's neck. "Never been surer of anything."

"What was it that made you… change your mind?"

"About leaving for Vermont and some ungodly snowy place, instead of staying here in the open air and sunshine with you?" Evan smiled cheekily. "Your big heart."

Heat immediately burst in Josh's cheeks. He cleared his throat, thinking of ice cubes, but he knew he was blushing. He grumbled under his breath.

"Helping Kev? Especially helping Adam? And helping me? That's the kind of guy I want to be with. The guy whose heart is big enough for everyone around him."

Josh squeezed Evan tightly. "I just like helping. Maybe I can use my own experience to help other people and do some good, you know?"

Evan nodded. "Like how? Hiring more people?"

"It doesn't always have to be a dude ranch," Josh murmured, rubbing Evan's chest and gazing off. "I've never told anyone this, but I've thought about shaking it up before. Making it some kind of… I don't know, foster home? Transitional housing? Something to help runaway LGBT teens? It sounds cheesy as shit…"

"It sounds exactly like you," Evan murmured, pressing a kiss against his neck. "Big-hearted. I'd love to do that kind of thing, I think."

"I just don't think I can be that kind of foster dad yet."

"Yet," Evan echoed, making Josh suddenly aware of his word choice.

"Yeah, well," Josh murmured, a smile tugging at his lips. "Dealing with those two will be an eye-opener, I think. After the mortgage is paid off, and I dip my toe in the water a little more, maybe. We'll see. And after I'm over my own... you know, issues."

Evan's thumb circling his chest, rubbing along every rib, calmed him enough to speak his mind. He'd never thought of himself as shy to do so before, but then, he'd kept secrets about his upbringing for long enough. "It'll be easier now that you're not hiding things," Evan murmured, echoing his own thoughts.

"Yeah. And now that I've got someone who..." Josh trailed off, gazing at Evan. He smiled broadly. "Who's worth the effort to heal."

Just like land took time to heal, it would take time for Josh to be ready for a different life. Depleted land needed different fertilizer—nutrients, oxygen, sunlight. Well, he'd had all of that, and he'd still never felt this hopeful about the future.

Maybe the missing ingredient, all along, had been simpler than he'd ever realized: unconditional love.

EVAN

EVAN SQUEEZED JOSH'S HAND UNDER THE TABLE AND BLINKED back the wetness from his eyes. As difficult as it was to say nothing, he was determined to let the brothers have their moment.

These people meant so much to Josh, and the fact that they'd welcomed him into their group without missing a beat meant a lot to Evan, too. And the way they were reacting to Josh finally telling them what he'd been hiding for years? Evan could have kissed them all, if their boyfriends weren't all around.

And if he weren't utterly, madly, head over heels in love with Josh. Just like he'd said, not even a month ago, in the best and worst moment of being overheard in his life. No, maybe the best was when Leo had heard what was going on with him and Monty and told Josh to come find him.

"I'm glad you could finally tell us." Tyler looked like the kind of guy who was rarely serious, but he was having a moment now. He leaned across Evan to punch Josh's arm. "I wish it could've been years ago."

Nobody seemed to quite be breathing, as if afraid to disturb it. Evan hardly dared move. Unbeknownst to anyone but Evan, Josh's hands—which had been trembling lightly—finally stilled.

"Me, too." Josh's voice was thick. "But better late than never."

"Hell, yeah." Nico folded his arms. "Whatever he said, you're a hell of a good guy to know."

"And to date," Evan interjected with a small smile.

Leo grinned. "And to work with, by all accounts."

"Oh, fuck off," Josh told them all, which stirred laughter. "I don't need the ego-stroking."

"No, I reckon Evan's got all the stroking you need under control." Oscar winked at them. Another round of laughter followed, this one louder. "More drinks?"

Josh grinned. "Nah, we gotta be heading back."

"What? Already?" Roman complained. "And all of us are together, too. And you'll miss the Pinterest board sharing." He cast Deen a meaningful look, which made Evan laugh. Wedding planning mode was in full swing.

"We've got an early morning. I gotta get some shit done before I spend the day teaching Kev some of the office work to get it off my hands. He wants to move to New York City. Wants more employable skills."

"Poor guy," Evan muttered under his breath, grinning. He was kind of excited for the kid, but he was glad as hell that it wasn't him.

The last few weeks had reinforced his decision to stay here. No way in hell would he be happier anywhere but right here, in the dirt and the sunshine and the misty foothills of the mountain range that he and Josh had yet to explore together.

All in good time.

As they said their goodbyes, with hugs and cheek-kisses all around, Evan took Josh's hand again to lead him outside. "Are you escaping more wedding talk?"

"Maybe," Josh grinned. "Didn't want you getting ideas. I want those back fields plowed and planted better before our summer wedding."

Evan giggled and snorted. "Plowed."

"You dirty man," Josh added, laughing as he kept a lookout for their Uber. "For the scenic backdrop, of course."

Oh my God, he's planning the flowers already. Evan's grin was so wide he could barely contain it. "Mmhmm. You can plow and plant your seeds in my back fields every day."

Josh laughed and squeezed his hand. "I'll take you up on that."

A comfortable silence fell between them as they stood closer together for warmth. The autumn evenings were getting chilly now, but Evan was looking forward to seeing what winter here was like.

"Huh," Josh murmured under his breath.

"Hm?"

Josh hesitated, but at last, he answered. "They were great about it, tonight. Maybe I was all worked up over nothing. I'd been going and thinking that I needed to find love, but… they love me."

The love all the guys had for each other was like nothing Evan had experienced. He'd instantly made ten new best friends, and he couldn't have felt more at home amongst them. "Yeah, they really do."

"Maybe I wasn't waiting for love. Maybe I was waiting to be ready for it."

Evan lost his breath all of a sudden. "That's the

damnedest thing. That's just how I feel." He squeezed Josh's hand and tipped his head back, squinting through the lights of the city to see the stars.

It felt like the future was smiling at them. Even in the autumn chill, they didn't tremble. They stood close, sharing their heat to stay warm.

Warm, happy, and together.

Hard Hart

HART'S BAY #1

"I FELT WRONG UNTIL I MET YOU."

Jesse is rebuilding his life. He's ditched his no-good ex, sworn off men, moved to a new town with his four best friends, and started the pottery business of his dreams. And then he slept with his hunky new neighbor. Oops.

Trouble just blew into town. Finn Hart knows that building a life with Jesse will reignite tensions in a town founded by one Hart, and slowly being strangled by another—Finn's grandfather. The construction foreman just can't stay away.

Saving Hart's Bay begins with encouraging tourism. Opening Jesse's new art gallery would be a great start, but not everyone wants change. Can Finn and Jesse's love wash away twenty years of bad blood and bring a new dawn for everyone?

Hard Hart is the first book in the Hart's Bay series about a small town full of seaside lovers and nosy but well-meaning neighbors. It can be read on its own, and promises a happily-ever-after ending and plenty of smiles and steam along the way. If that cove could talk... oh boy, has it ever seen things.

Independent Publisher Book Awards 2020 - Silver Medalist for LGBT+ Fiction

Rainbow Awards Honorable Mention

Also by E. Davies

Sunrise Island Brothers:

Collide

Stranded

Hart's Bay:

Hard Hart

Changed Hart

Wild Hart

Stolen Hart

Significant Brothers:

Splinter

Grasp

Slick

Trace

Clutch

Tremble

Riley Brothers:

Buzz

Clang

Swish

Crunch

Slam

Grind

Brooklyn Boys:

Electric Sunshine

Live Wire

Boiling Point

F-Word:

Flaunt

Freak

Faux

Forever

Freedom

After:

Afterburn

Afterglow

Aftermath

Shared Universes:

Shelter

Adore

Miracle

Redemption

Limelight

Barely Regal

www.ingramcontent.com/pod-product-compliance
Lightning Source LLC
Chambersburg PA
CBHW050844190726
48286CB00007B/2226